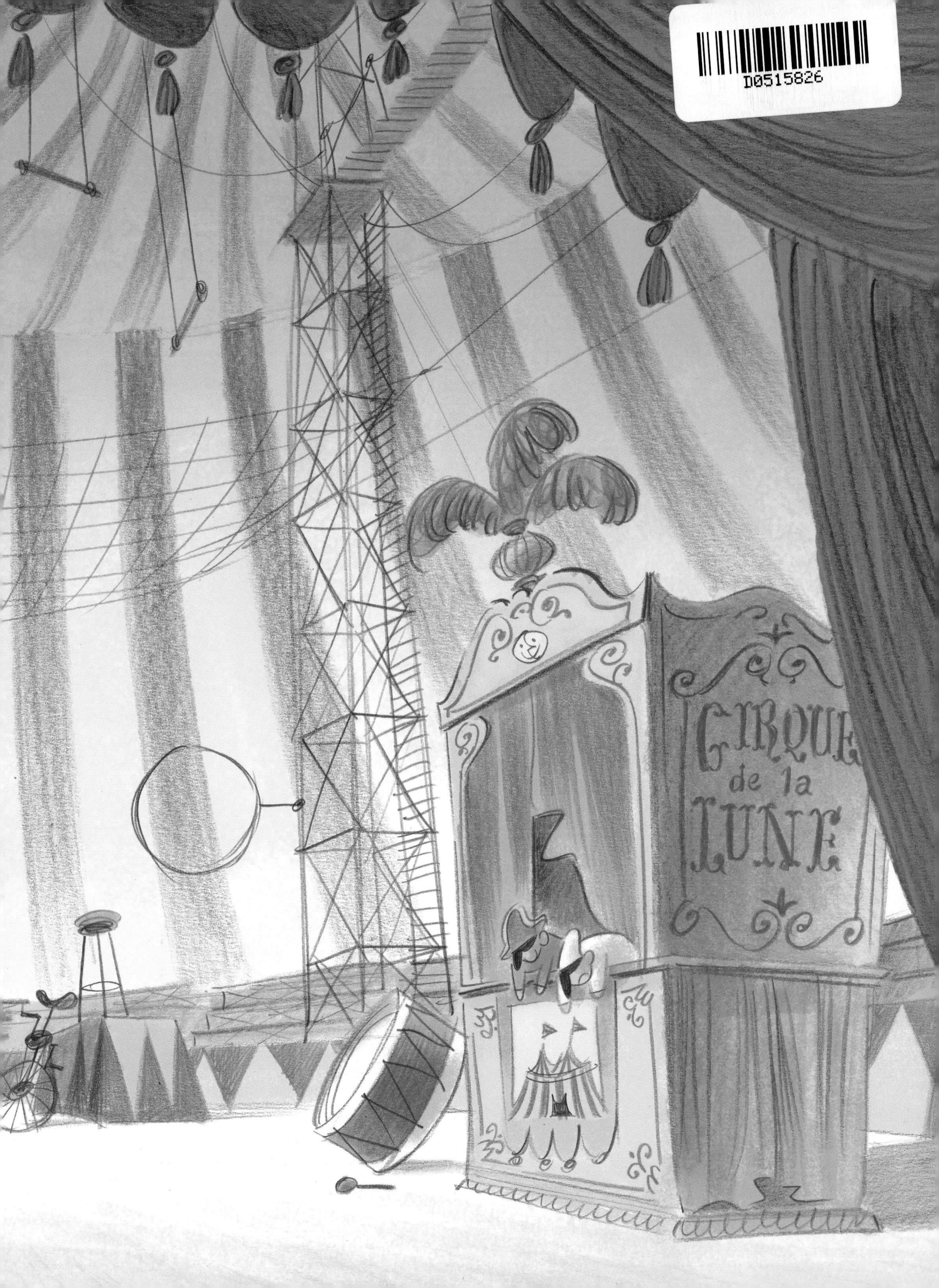
CIRQUE
de la
LUNE

"MAYBE MY HEAD IS OFTEN IN THE CLOUDS BECAUSE, LIKE THEM, I'M ALWAYS TRAVELING AND I DON'T KNOW WHERE THE WIND WILL TAKE ME...

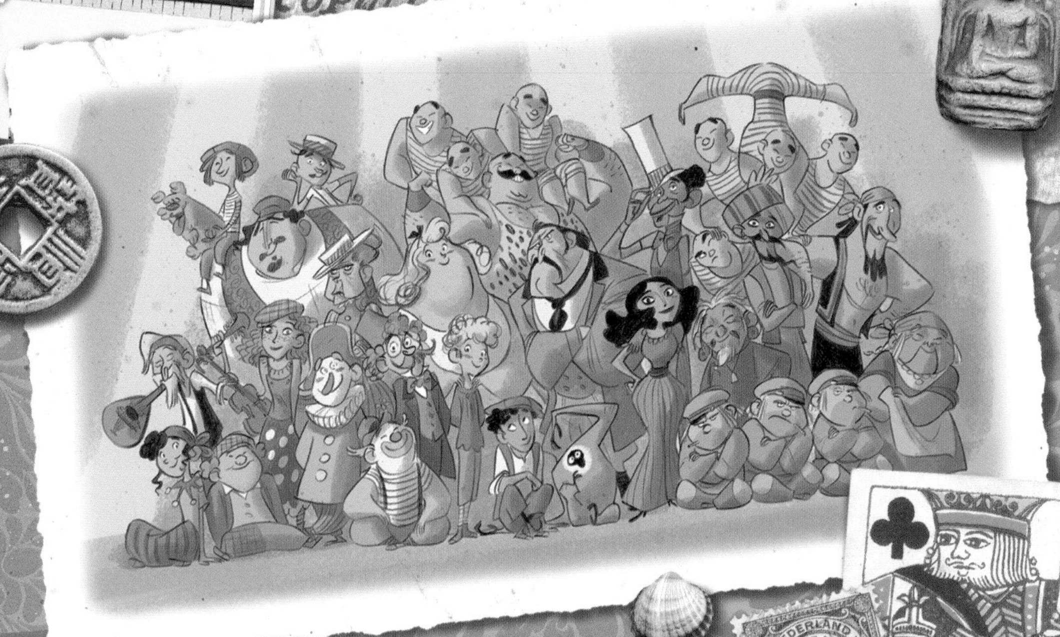

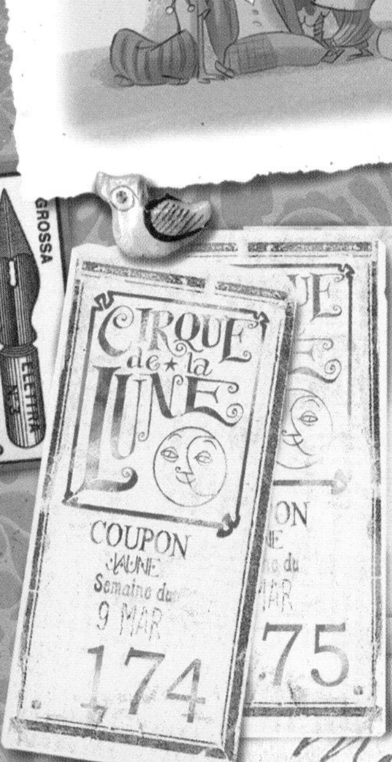
CIRQUE de la LUNE
COUPON
JAUNE
9 MAR
174
75

"MY NAME IS VIOLETTE VERMEER-- DUTCH FATHER, FRENCH MOTHER... CITIZEN OF THE WORLD!"

TERESA RADICE ★ STEFANO TURCONI

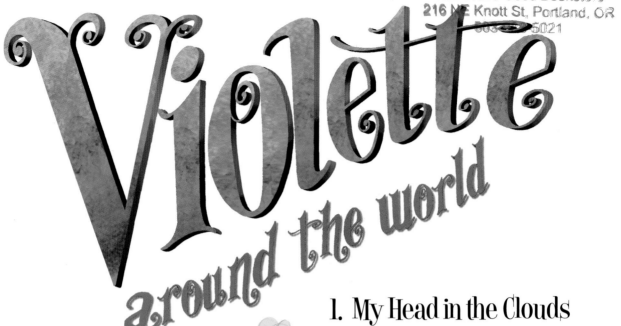

Violette around the world

1. My Head in the Clouds

EURO COMICS
ENGLISH EDITION   GRAPHIC NOVELS

An imprint of IDW PUBLISHING

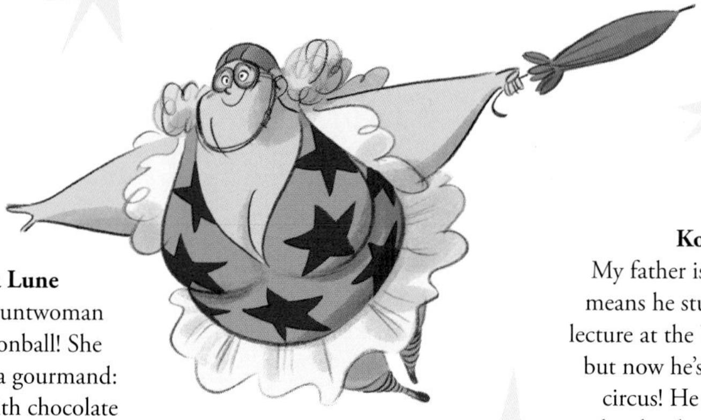

Amélie de la Lune
My mother is a stuntwoman and human cannonball! She is super sweet and a gourmand: she loves waffles with chocolate on top! She also sews beautiful patchwork quilts for people she likes.

Konrad Vermeer
My father is an entomologist. That means he studies insects! He used to lecture at the University of Amsterdam, but now he's the insect trainer in the circus! He always has his head in the clouds. (Which must be where I get it from!)

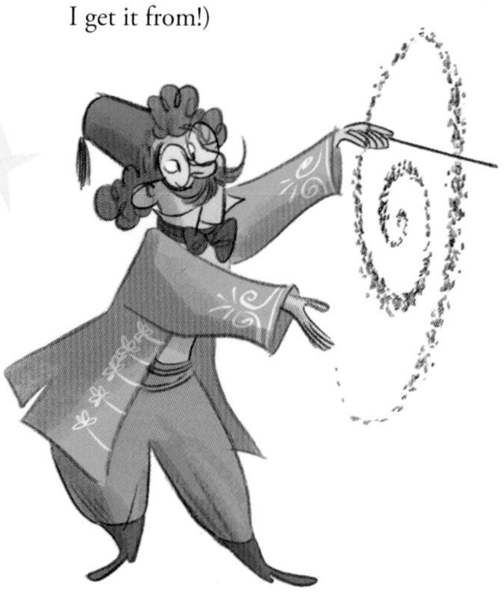

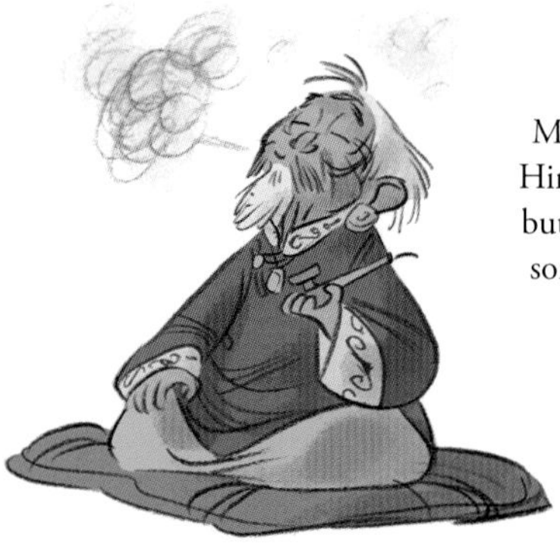

Grandad Tenzin
My grandfather was born in the Himalayas. He doesn't talk much, but when he does, it really means something. He is a great teacher and has infinite patience. He's a wise man!

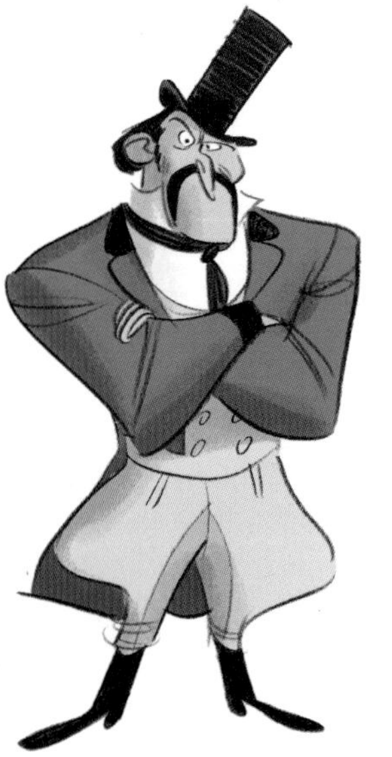

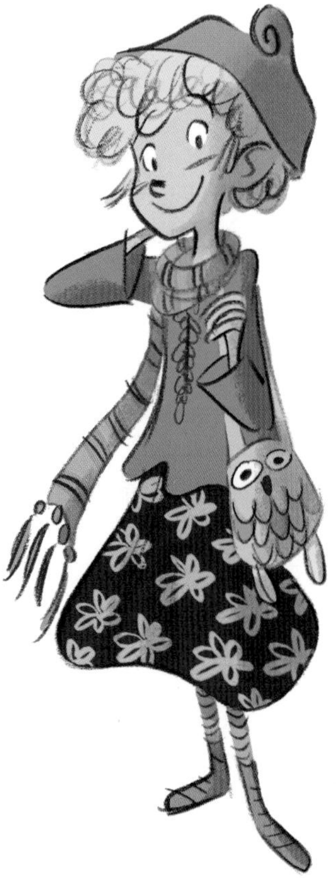

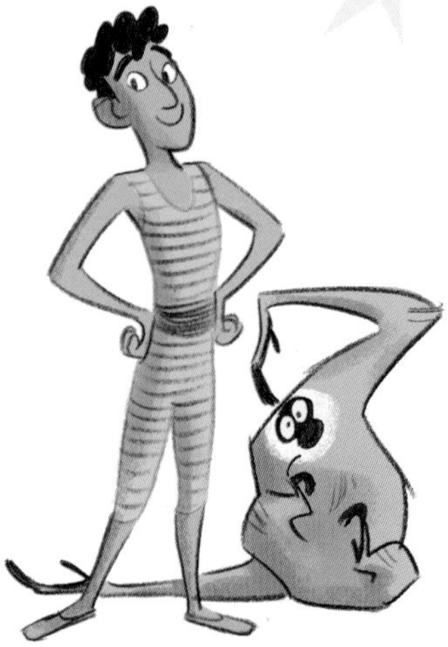

Arsène de la Lune
Ah! My uncle Arsène! He looks grumpy, doesn't he? He's the director of our circus. When it comes down to it, though (and I swear to it!), he has a heart of gold.

Samir and Sindbad
Samir is my best friend, he's two years older than me and he's a trapeze artist, like his big sister Fatima. They come from Damascus, just like Sindbad, their gibbon who follows Samir everywhere he goes!

Violette
…and here I am, Violette Vermeer, almost twelve years old. I love to travel and I'm curious about everything, always looking for the beauty in the world.

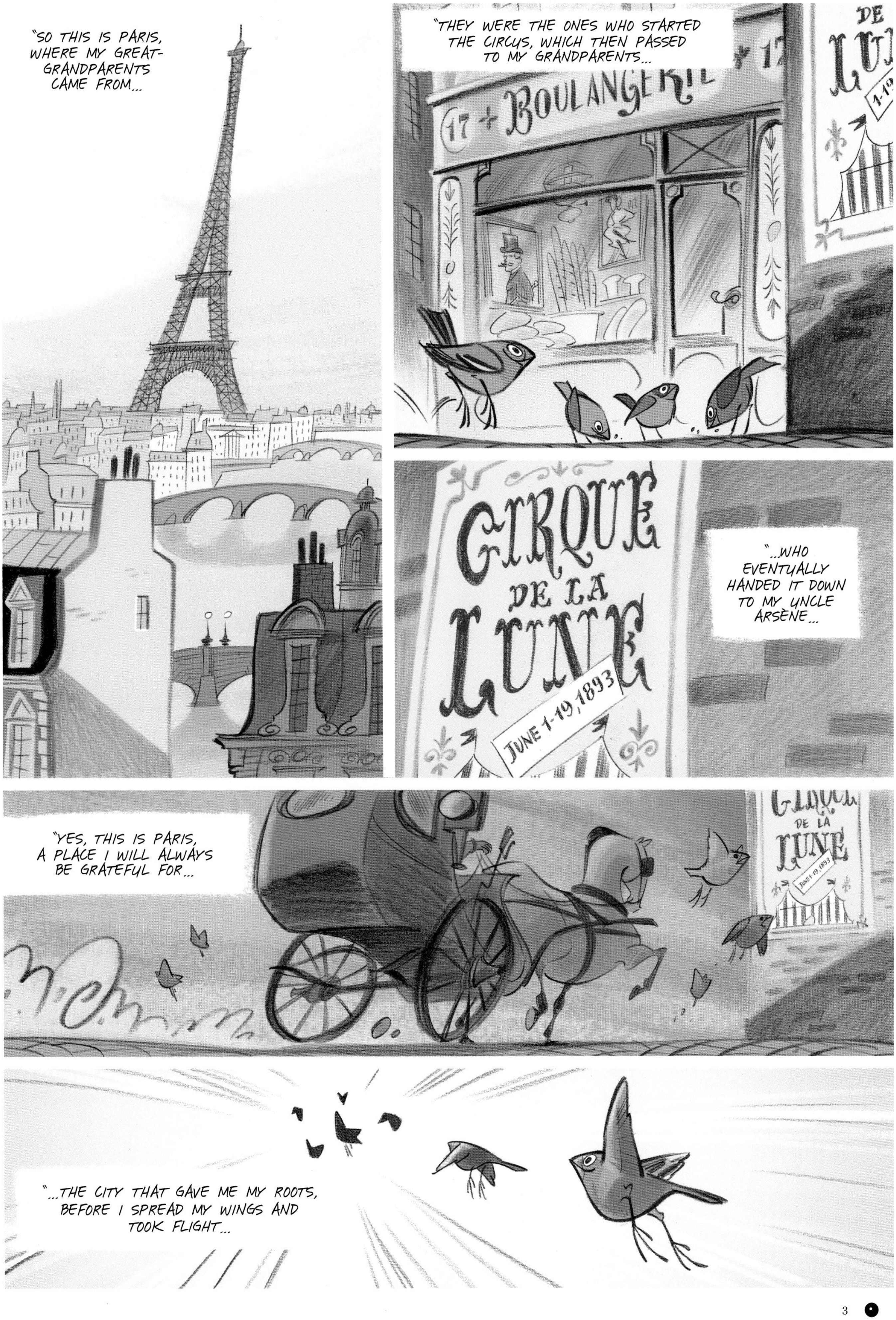
"SO THIS IS PARIS, WHERE MY GREAT-GRANDPARENTS CAME FROM...
"THEY WERE THE ONES WHO STARTED THE CIRCUS, WHICH THEN PASSED TO MY GRANDPARENTS...
17 + BOULANGERIE
CIRQUE DE LA LUNE
JUNE 1-19, 1893
"...WHO EVENTUALLY HANDED IT DOWN TO MY UNCLE ARSÈNE...
"YES, THIS IS PARIS, A PLACE I WILL ALWAYS BE GRATEFUL FOR...
CIRQUE DE LA LUNE
JUNE 1-19, 1893
"...THE CITY THAT GAVE ME MY ROOTS, BEFORE I SPREAD MY WINGS AND TOOK FLIGHT...

"...SO WHY DO I WANT TO BE SOMEWHERE ELSE? WELL..."

...AND THEREFORE, STUDENTS, IT WAS ONLY IN THE MIDDLE OF THE ELEVENTH CENTURY THAT LITERATURE PROPER BEGAN...

SCHOOL

AT THAT TIME, OUR COUNTRY WAS DIVIDED INTO TWO SEPARATE PARTS -- THE NORTH, WHERE THEY SPOKE **LANGUE D'OIL**, FROM WHICH MODERN FRENCH DEVELOPED...

HEY, BIRDIE, WANNA SNACK?

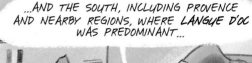

...AND THE SOUTH, INCLUDING PROVENCE AND NEARBY REGIONS, WHERE **LANGUE D'OC** WAS PREDOMINANT...

PARIS

FRANCE

HEY! WATCH OUT WITH THAT BEAK! WANNA TURN MY HAND INTO A STRAINER?

HAHAHA, YOUR FEET TICKLE!

BUT PERHAPS MISS VERMEER CAN EXPLAIN, SEEING AS SHE'S ALREADY BUSY CHATTERING...

...IN BIRD LANGUAGE!

GULP!

CHIRP?

SMACK

ISN'T THAT SO, MISS VERMEER?

I...I'M SORRY, MADAME! I DIDN'T THINK...

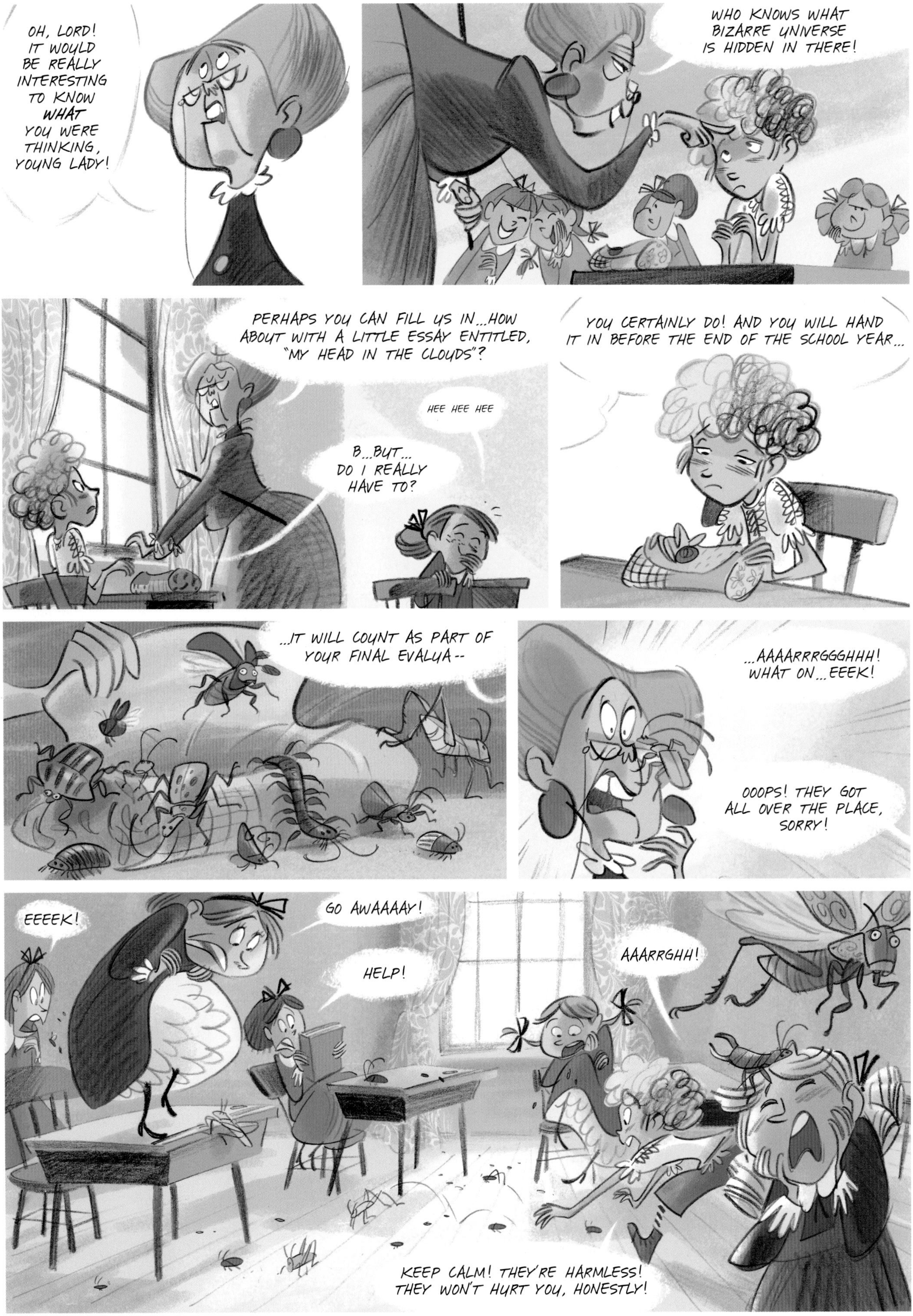
OH, LORD! IT WOULD BE REALLY INTERESTING TO KNOW WHAT YOU WERE THINKING, YOUNG LADY!
WHO KNOWS WHAT BIZARRE UNIVERSE IS HIDDEN IN THERE!
PERHAPS YOU CAN FILL US IN...HOW ABOUT WITH A LITTLE ESSAY ENTITLED, "MY HEAD IN THE CLOUDS"?
HEE HEE HEE
B...BUT... DO I REALLY HAVE TO?
YOU CERTAINLY DO! AND YOU WILL HAND IT IN BEFORE THE END OF THE SCHOOL YEAR...
...IT WILL COUNT AS PART OF YOUR FINAL EVALUA--
...AAAARRRGGGHHH! WHAT ON...EEEK!
OOOPS! THEY GOT ALL OVER THE PLACE, SORRY!
EEEEK!
GO AWAAAAY!
HELP!
AAARRGHH!
KEEP CALM! THEY'RE HARMLESS! THEY WON'T HURT YOU, HONESTLY!

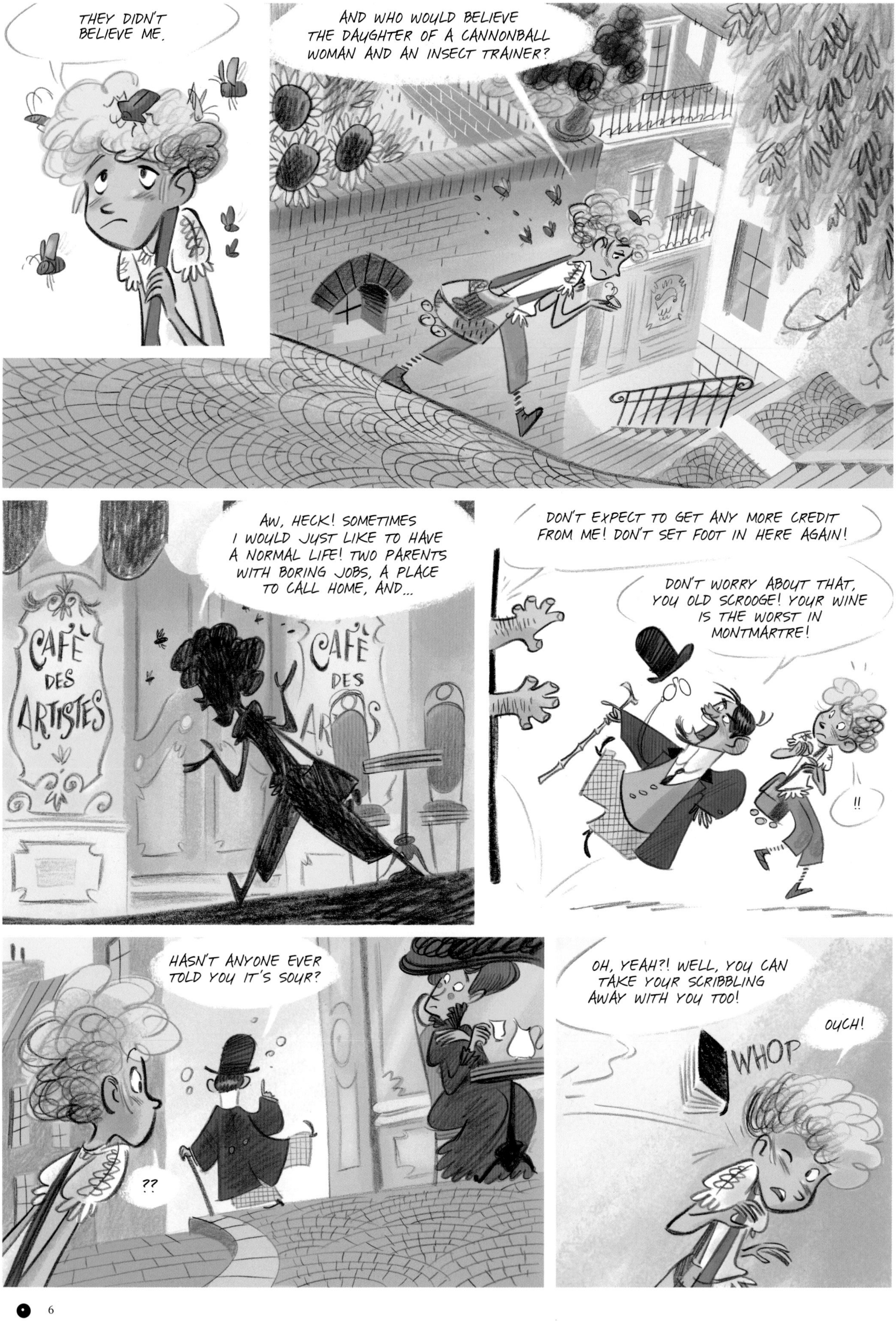
THEY DIDN'T BELIEVE ME.
AND WHO WOULD BELIEVE THE DAUGHTER OF A CANNONBALL WOMAN AND AN INSECT TRAINER?
AW, HECK! SOMETIMES I WOULD JUST LIKE TO HAVE A NORMAL LIFE! TWO PARENTS WITH BORING JOBS, A PLACE TO CALL HOME, AND...
CAFÉ DES ARTISTES
DON'T EXPECT TO GET ANY MORE CREDIT FROM ME! DON'T SET FOOT IN HERE AGAIN!
DON'T WORRY ABOUT THAT, YOU OLD SCROOGE! YOUR WINE IS THE WORST IN MONTMARTRE!
!!
HASN'T ANYONE EVER TOLD YOU IT'S SOUR?
??
OH, YEAH?! WELL, YOU CAN TAKE YOUR SCRIBBLING AWAY WITH YOU TOO!
WHOP
OUCH!

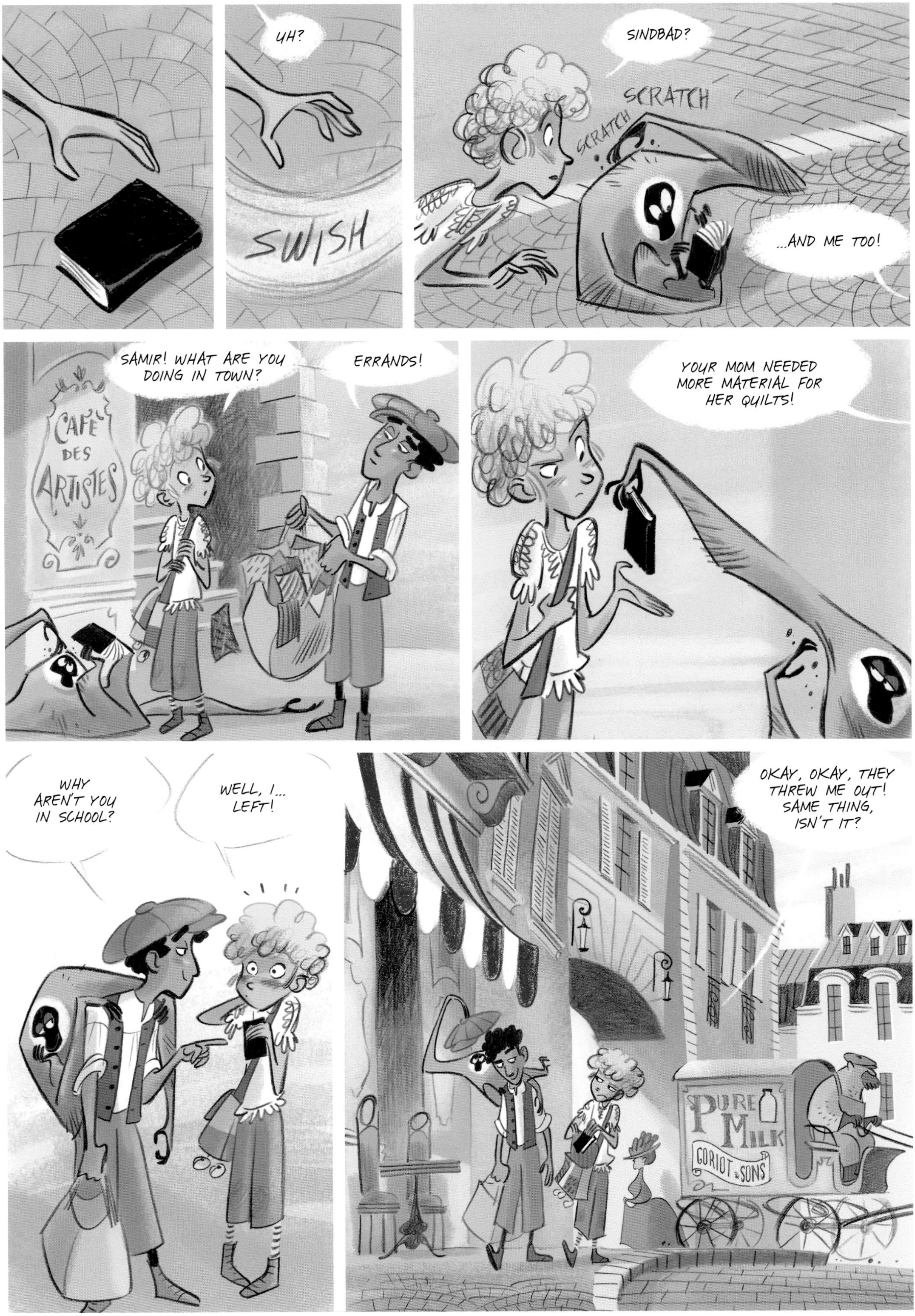

UH?
SWISH
SINDBAD?
SCRATCH
SCRATCH
...AND ME TOO!
SAMIR! WHAT ARE YOU DOING IN TOWN?
ERRANDS!
CAFÉ DES ARTISTES
YOUR MOM NEEDED MORE MATERIAL FOR HER QUILTS!
WHY AREN'T YOU IN SCHOOL?
WELL, I... LEFT!
OKAY, OKAY, THEY THREW ME OUT! SAME THING, ISN'T IT?
PURE MILK
GORIOT & SONS

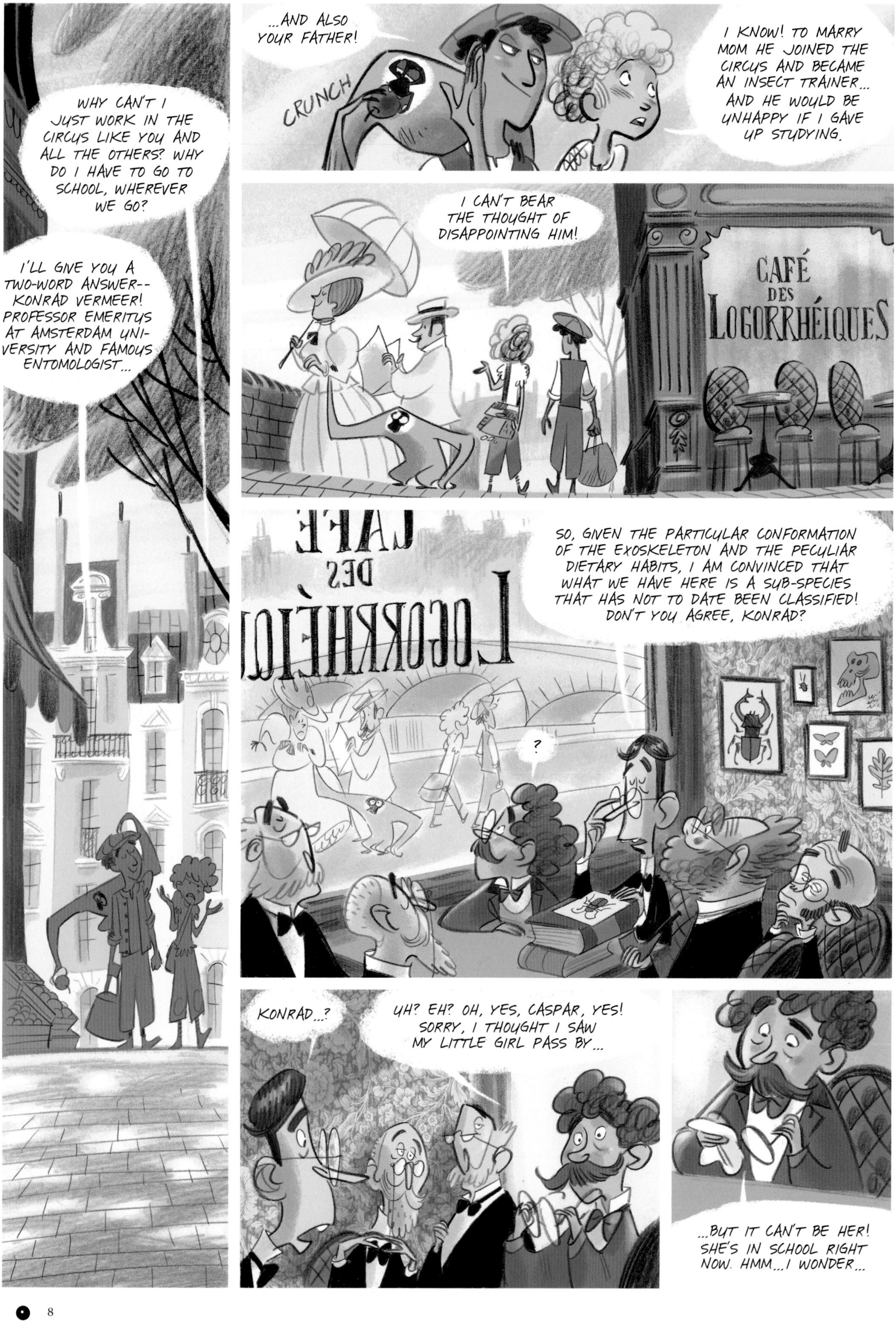
WHY CAN'T I JUST WORK IN THE CIRCUS LIKE YOU AND ALL THE OTHERS? WHY DO I HAVE TO GO TO SCHOOL, WHEREVER WE GO?
I'LL GIVE YOU A TWO-WORD ANSWER--KONRAD VERMEER! PROFESSOR EMERITUS AT AMSTERDAM UNIVERSITY AND FAMOUS ENTOMOLOGIST...
...AND ALSO YOUR FATHER!
CRUNCH
I KNOW! TO MARRY MOM HE JOINED THE CIRCUS AND BECAME AN INSECT TRAINER... AND HE WOULD BE UNHAPPY IF I GAVE UP STUDYING.
I CAN'T BEAR THE THOUGHT OF DISAPPOINTING HIM!
CAFÉ DES LOGORRHÉIQUES
SO, GIVEN THE PARTICULAR CONFORMATION OF THE EXOSKELETON AND THE PECULIAR DIETARY HABITS, I AM CONVINCED THAT WHAT WE HAVE HERE IS A SUB-SPECIES THAT HAS NOT TO DATE BEEN CLASSIFIED! DON'T YOU AGREE, KONRAD?
?
KONRAD...?
UH? EH? OH, YES, CASPAR, YES! SORRY, I THOUGHT I SAW MY LITTLE GIRL PASS BY...
...BUT IT CAN'T BE HER! SHE'S IN SCHOOL RIGHT NOW. HMM...I WONDER...

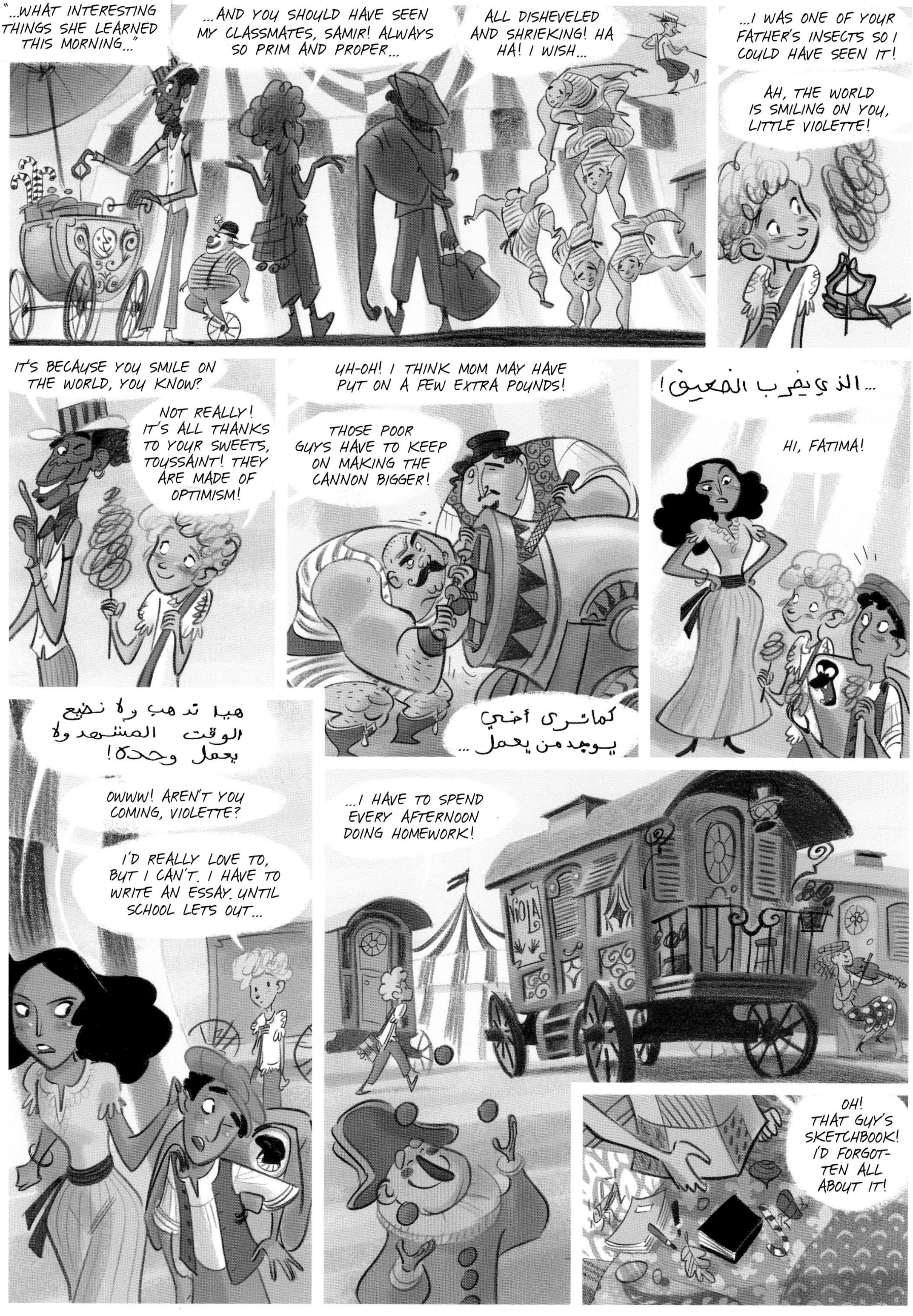
"...WHAT INTERESTING THINGS SHE LEARNED THIS MORNING..."
...AND YOU SHOULD HAVE SEEN MY CLASSMATES, SAMIR! ALWAYS SO PRIM AND PROPER...
ALL DISHEVELED AND SHRIEKING! HA HA! I WISH...
...I WAS ONE OF YOUR FATHER'S INSECTS SO I COULD HAVE SEEN IT!
AH, THE WORLD IS SMILING ON YOU, LITTLE VIOLETTE!
IT'S BECAUSE YOU SMILE ON THE WORLD, YOU KNOW?
NOT REALLY! IT'S ALL THANKS TO YOUR SWEETS, TOUSSAINT! THEY ARE MADE OF OPTIMISM!
UH-OH! I THINK MOM MAY HAVE PUT ON A FEW EXTRA POUNDS!
THOSE POOR GUYS HAVE TO KEEP ON MAKING THE CANNON BIGGER!
كما ترى أختي يوجد من يعمل ...
...الذي يضرب الضعيف!
HI, FATIMA!
هيا تذهب ولا نضيع الوقت المشهد ولا يعمل وحده!
OWWW! AREN'T YOU COMING, VIOLETTE?
I'D REALLY LOVE TO, BUT I CAN'T. I HAVE TO WRITE AN ESSAY. UNTIL SCHOOL LETS OUT...
...I HAVE TO SPEND EVERY AFTERNOON DOING HOMEWORK!
VIOLA
OH! THAT GUY'S SKETCHBOOK! I'D FORGOT-TEN ALL ABOUT IT!

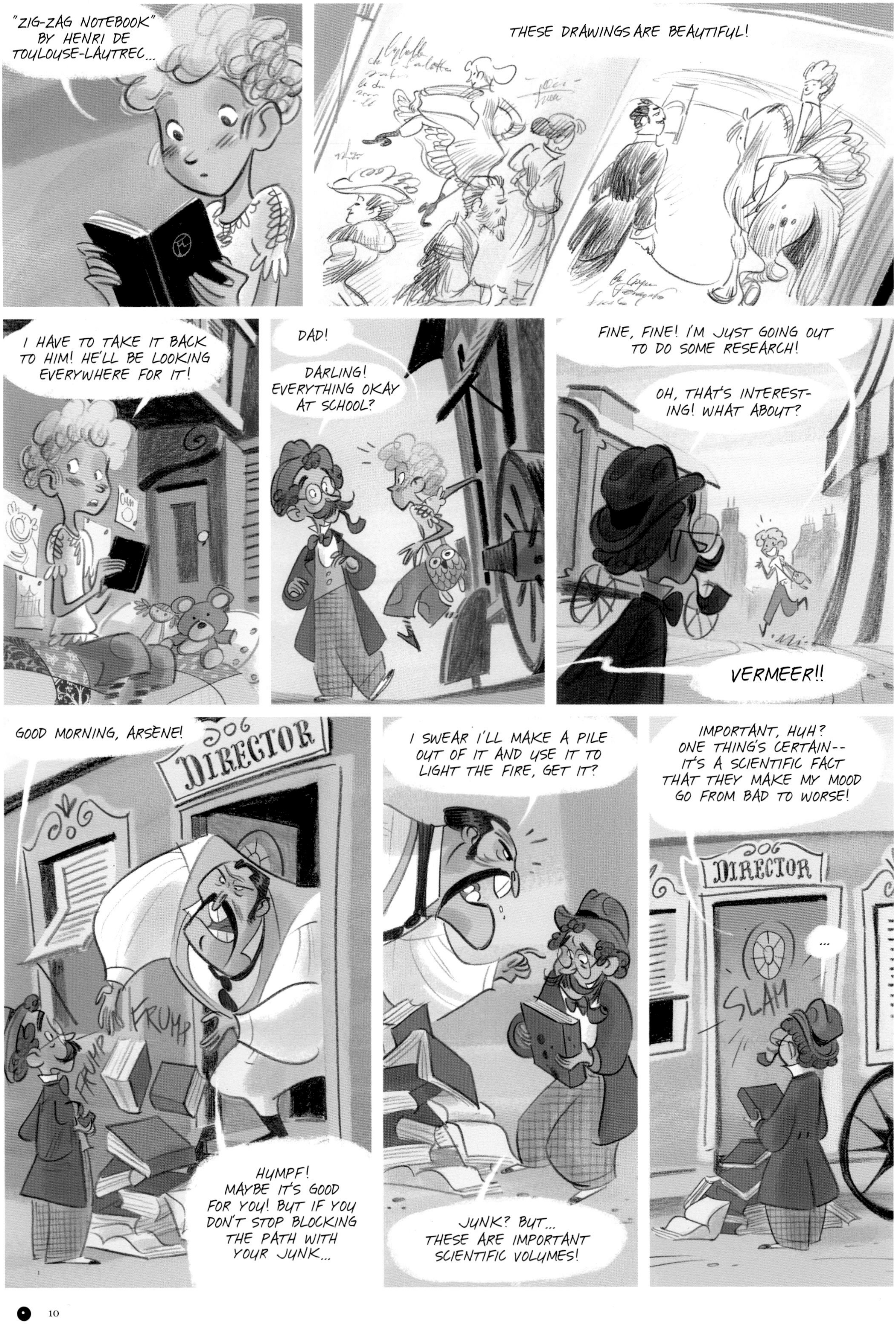
"ZIG-ZAG NOTEBOOK" BY HENRI DE TOULOUSE-LAUTREC...
THESE DRAWINGS ARE BEAUTIFUL!
I HAVE TO TAKE IT BACK TO HIM! HE'LL BE LOOKING EVERYWHERE FOR IT!
DAD!
DARLING! EVERYTHING OKAY AT SCHOOL?
FINE, FINE! I'M JUST GOING OUT TO DO SOME RESEARCH!
OH, THAT'S INTEREST-ING! WHAT ABOUT?
VERMEER!!
GOOD MORNING, ARSÈNE!
DIRECTOR
FRUMP
FRUMP
FRUMP
HUMPF! MAYBE IT'S GOOD FOR YOU! BUT IF YOU DON'T STOP BLOCKING THE PATH WITH YOUR JUNK...
I SWEAR I'LL MAKE A PILE OUT OF IT AND USE IT TO LIGHT THE FIRE, GET IT?
JUNK? BUT... THESE ARE IMPORTANT SCIENTIFIC VOLUMES!
IMPORTANT, HUH? ONE THING'S CERTAIN-- IT'S A SCIENTIFIC FACT THAT THEY MAKE MY MOOD GO FROM BAD TO WORSE!
DIRECTOR
...
SLAM

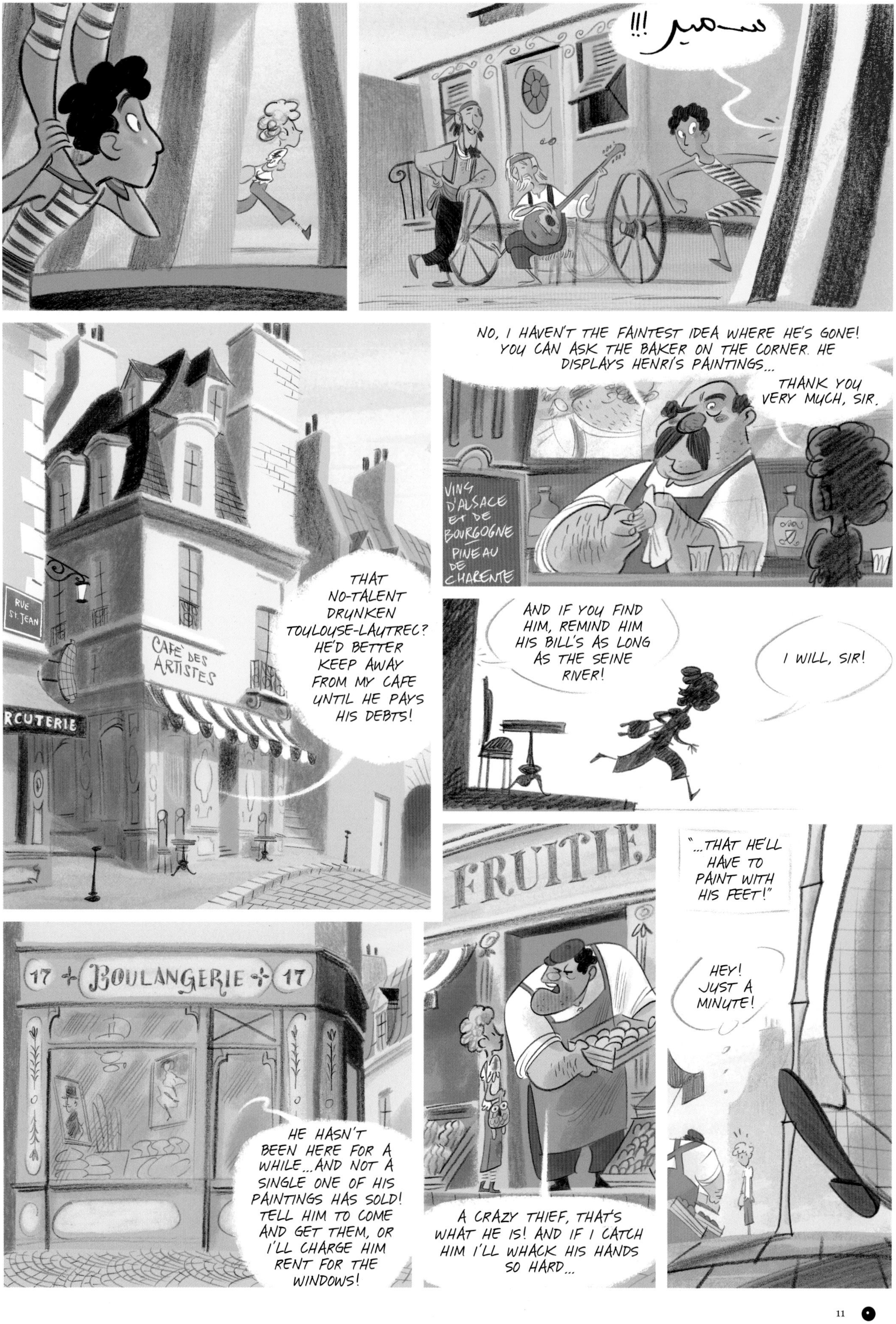
سمير!!!
RUE ST JEAN
CAFÉ DES ARTISTES
RCUTERIE
THAT NO-TALENT DRUNKEN TOULOUSE-LAUTREC? HE'D BETTER KEEP AWAY FROM MY CAFE UNTIL HE PAYS HIS DEBTS!
NO, I HAVEN'T THE FAINTEST IDEA WHERE HE'S GONE! YOU CAN ASK THE BAKER ON THE CORNER. HE DISPLAYS HENRI'S PAINTINGS...
THANK YOU VERY MUCH, SIR.
VINS D'ALSACE ET DE BOURGOGNE PINEAU DE CHARENTE
AND IF YOU FIND HIM, REMIND HIM HIS BILL'S AS LONG AS THE SEINE RIVER!
I WILL, SIR!
17 BOULANGERIE 17
HE HASN'T BEEN HERE FOR A WHILE... AND NOT A SINGLE ONE OF HIS PAINTINGS HAS SOLD! TELL HIM TO COME AND GET THEM, OR I'LL CHARGE HIM RENT FOR THE WINDOWS!
FRUITIE
A CRAZY THIEF, THAT'S WHAT HE IS! AND IF I CATCH HIM I'LL WHACK HIS HANDS SO HARD...
"...THAT HE'LL HAVE TO PAINT WITH HIS FEET!"
HEY! JUST A MINUTE!

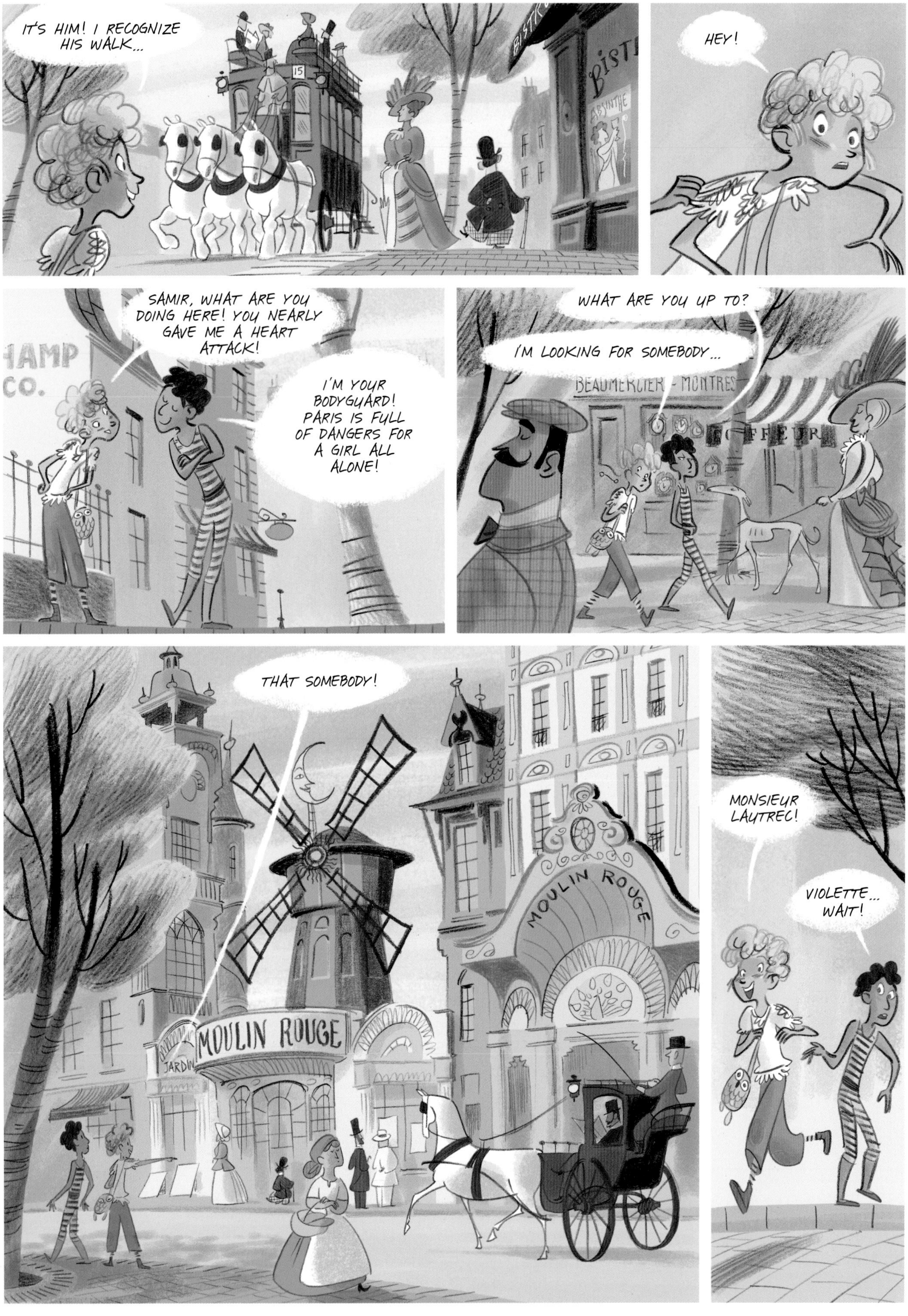
IT'S HIM! I RECOGNIZE HIS WALK...
BISTRO
ABSINTHE
HEY!
SAMIR, WHAT ARE YOU DOING HERE! YOU NEARLY GAVE ME A HEART ATTACK!
I'M YOUR BODYGUARD! PARIS IS FULL OF DANGERS FOR A GIRL ALL ALONE!
WHAT ARE YOU UP TO?
I'M LOOKING FOR SOMEBODY...
BEAUMERCIER - MONTRES
THAT SOMEBODY!
MOULIN ROUGE
JARDIN
MOULIN ROUGE
MONSIEUR LAUTREC!
VIOLETTE... WAIT!

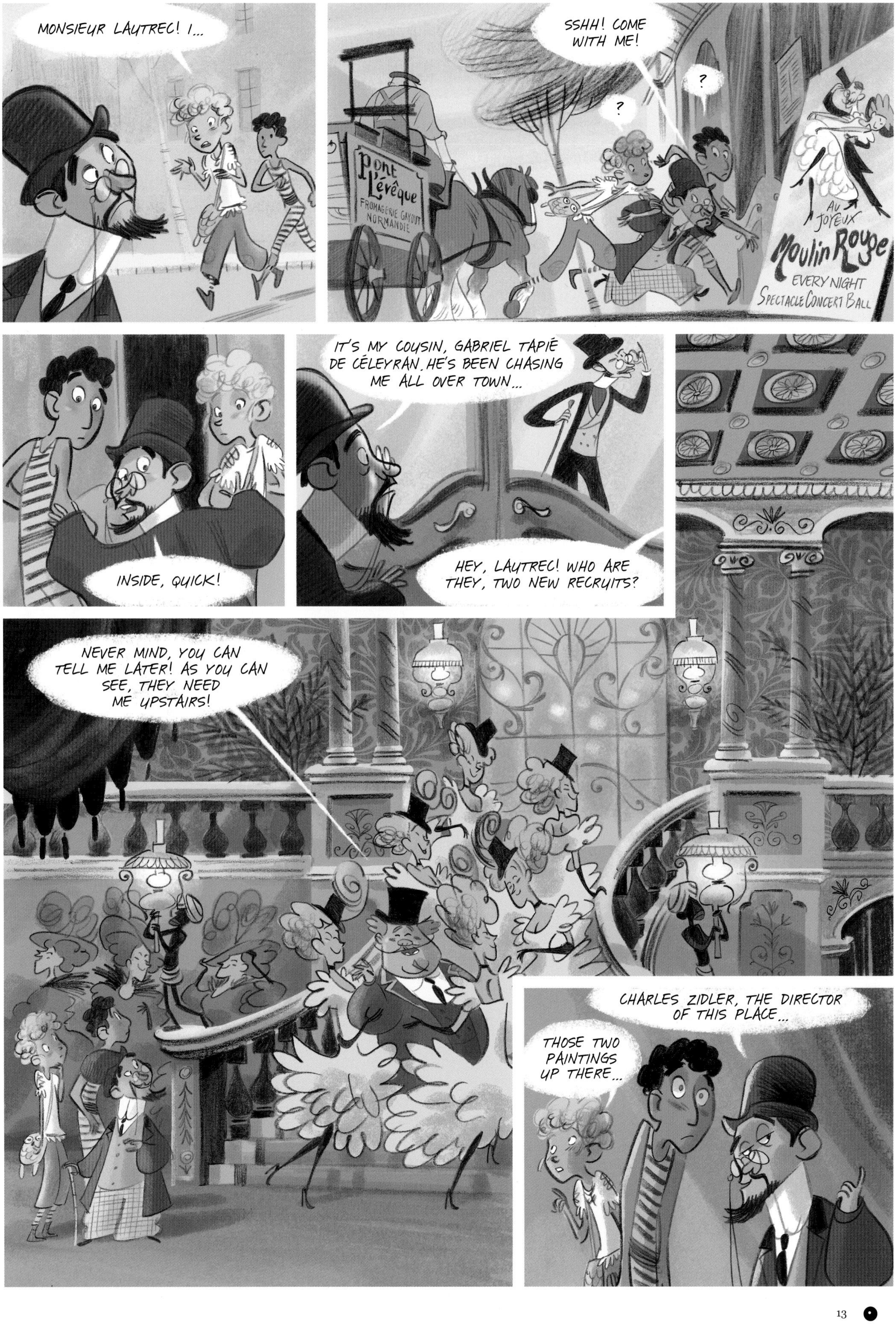
MONSIEUR LAUTREC! I...
SSHH! COME WITH ME!
?
?
Pont L'Évêque
FROMAGERIE GAYOUT NORMANDIE
AU JOYEUX Moulin Rouge
EVERY NIGHT
SPECTACLE CONCERT BALL
INSIDE, QUICK!
IT'S MY COUSIN, GABRIEL TAPIÉ DE CÉLEYRAN. HE'S BEEN CHASING ME ALL OVER TOWN...
HEY, LAUTREC! WHO ARE THEY, TWO NEW RECRUITS?
NEVER MIND, YOU CAN TELL ME LATER! AS YOU CAN SEE, THEY NEED ME UPSTAIRS!
CHARLES ZIDLER, THE DIRECTOR OF THIS PLACE...
THOSE TWO PAINTINGS UP THERE...

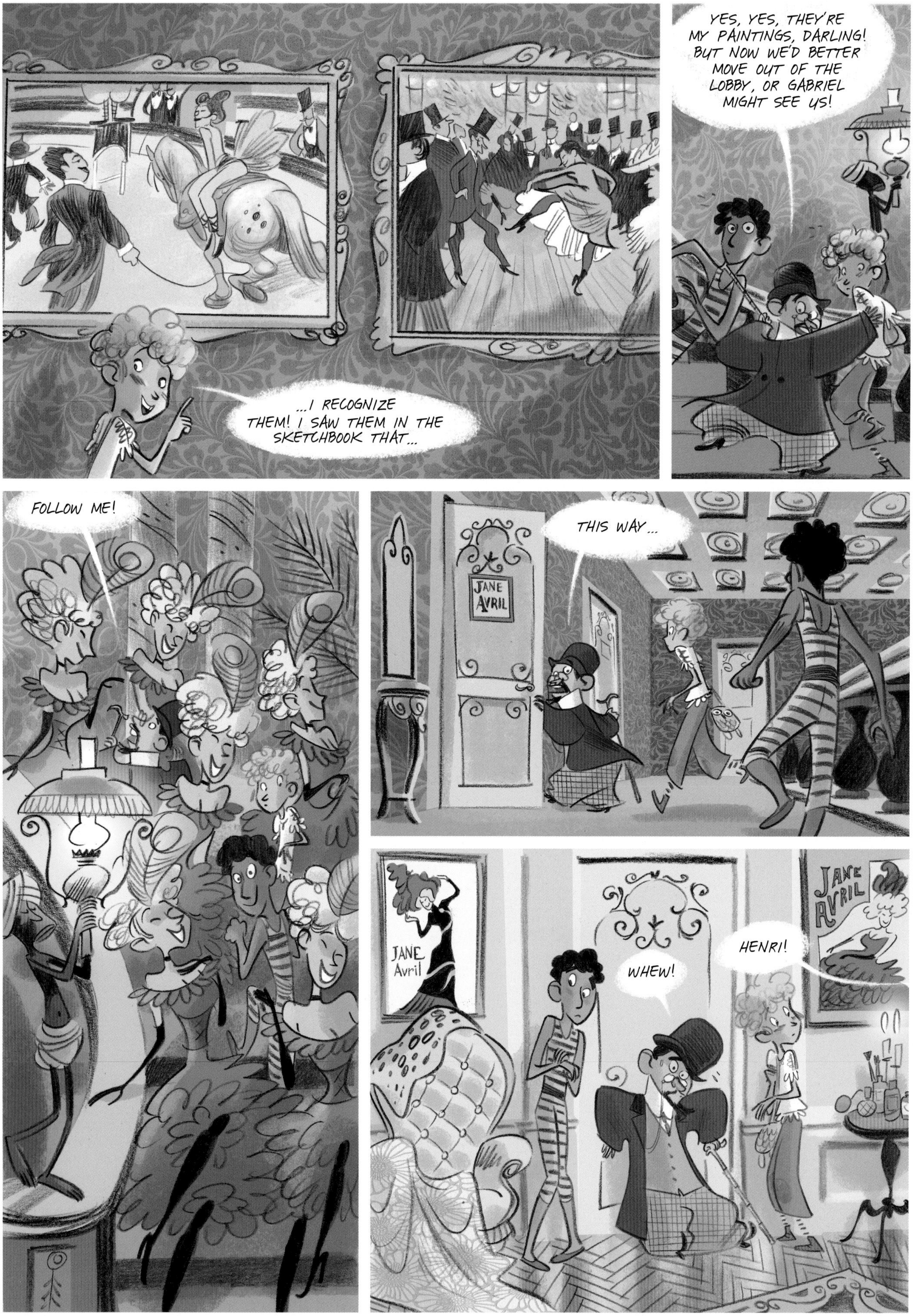
...I RECOGNIZE THEM! I SAW THEM IN THE SKETCHBOOK THAT...
YES, YES, THEY'RE MY PAINTINGS, DARLING! BUT NOW WE'D BETTER MOVE OUT OF THE LOBBY, OR GABRIEL MIGHT SEE US!
FOLLOW ME!
THIS WAY...
JANE AVRIL
JANE Avril
JANE AVRIL
WHEW!
HENRI!

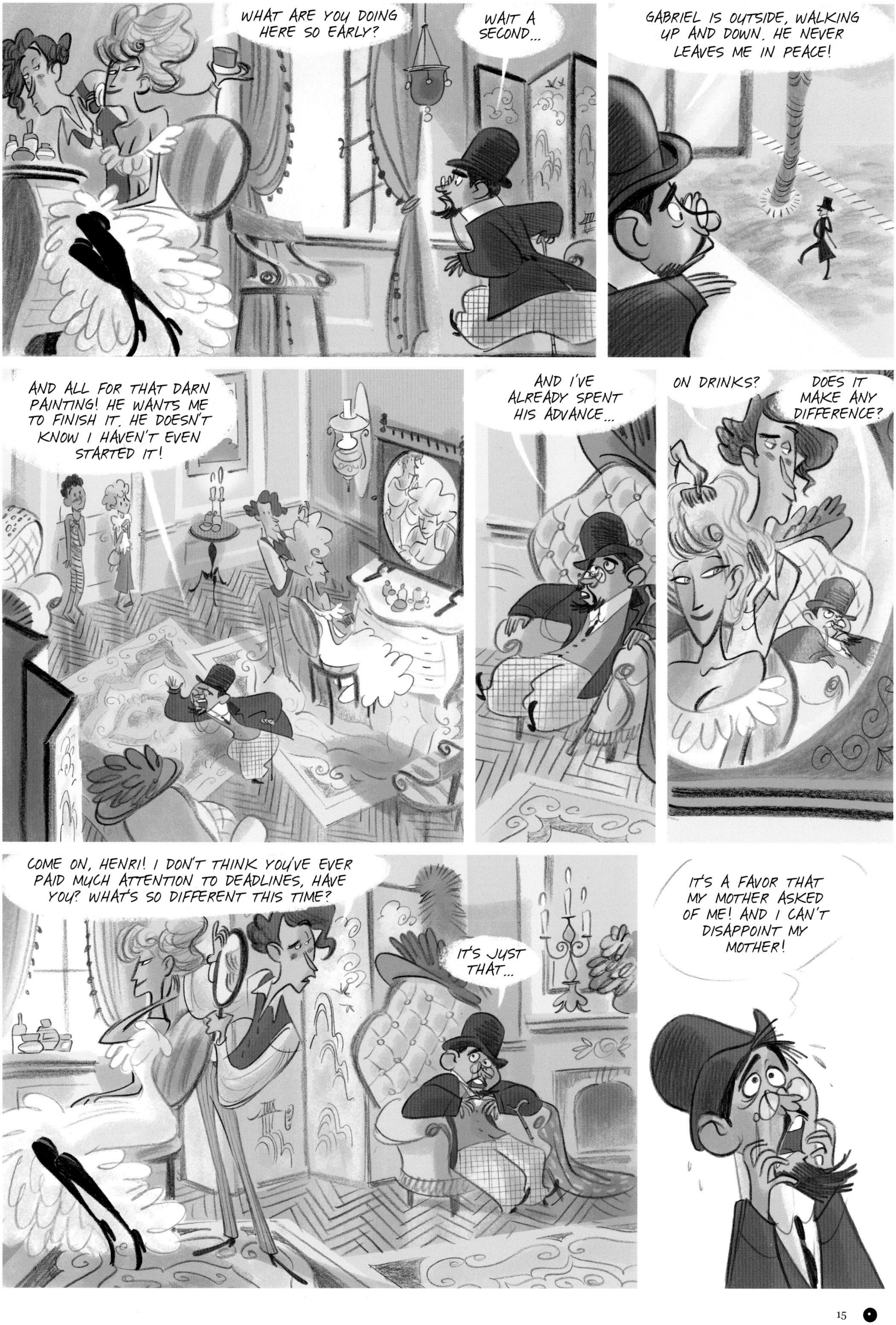
WHAT ARE YOU DOING HERE SO EARLY?
WAIT A SECOND...
GABRIEL IS OUTSIDE, WALKING UP AND DOWN. HE NEVER LEAVES ME IN PEACE!
AND ALL FOR THAT DARN PAINTING! HE WANTS ME TO FINISH IT. HE DOESN'T KNOW I HAVEN'T EVEN STARTED IT!
AND I'VE ALREADY SPENT HIS ADVANCE...
ON DRINKS?
DOES IT MAKE ANY DIFFERENCE?
COME ON, HENRI! I DON'T THINK YOU'VE EVER PAID MUCH ATTENTION TO DEADLINES, HAVE YOU? WHAT'S SO DIFFERENT THIS TIME?
IT'S JUST THAT...
IT'S A FAVOR THAT MY MOTHER ASKED OF ME! AND I CAN'T DISAPPOINT MY MOTHER!

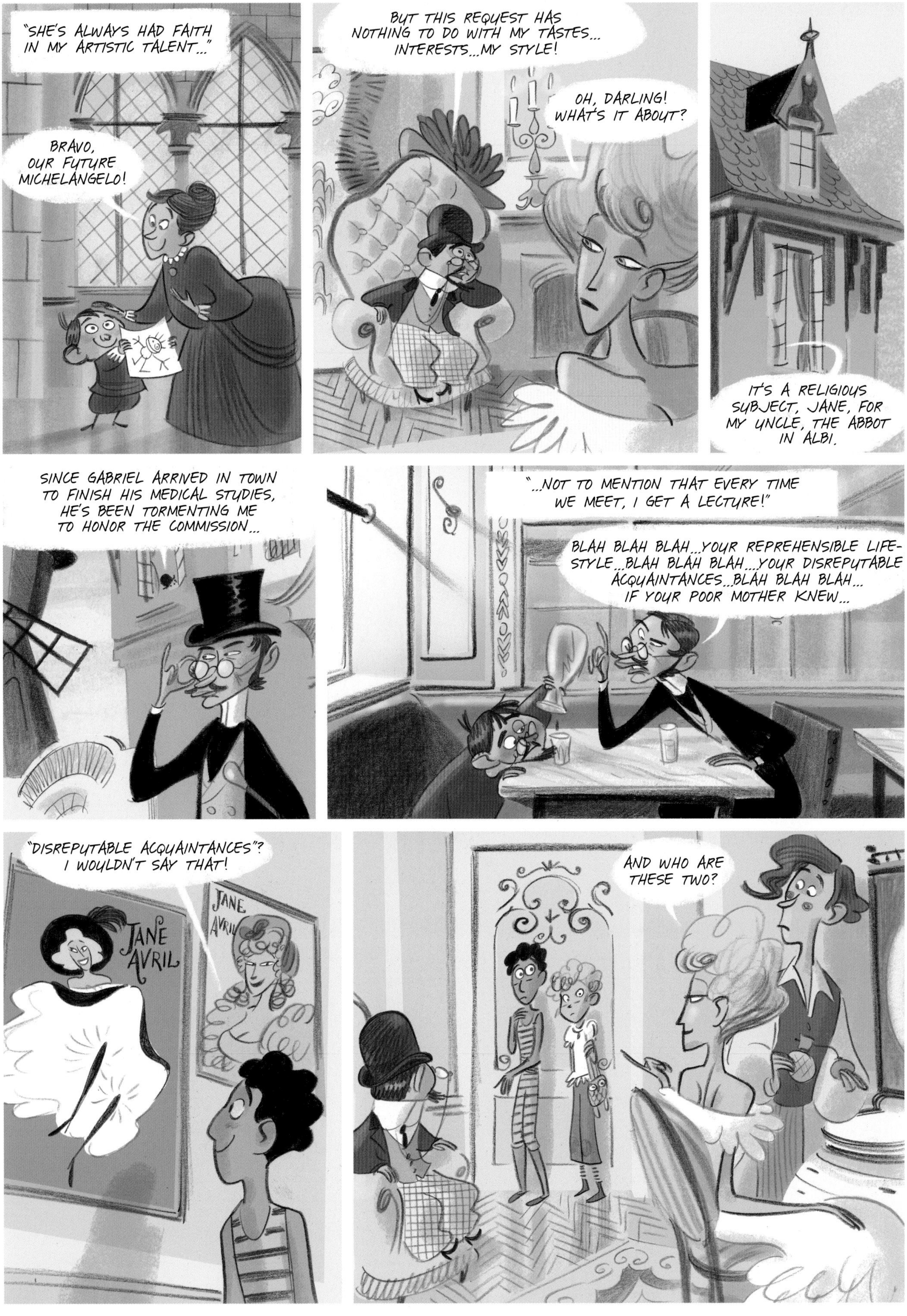
"SHE'S ALWAYS HAD FAITH IN MY ARTISTIC TALENT..."
BRAVO, OUR FUTURE MICHELANGELO!
BUT THIS REQUEST HAS NOTHING TO DO WITH MY TASTES... INTERESTS...MY STYLE!
OH, DARLING! WHAT'S IT ABOUT?
IT'S A RELIGIOUS SUBJECT, JANE, FOR MY UNCLE, THE ABBOT IN ALBI.
SINCE GABRIEL ARRIVED IN TOWN TO FINISH HIS MEDICAL STUDIES, HE'S BEEN TORMENTING ME TO HONOR THE COMMISSION...
"...NOT TO MENTION THAT EVERY TIME WE MEET, I GET A LECTURE!"
BLAH BLAH BLAH...YOUR REPREHENSIBLE LIFE-STYLE...BLAH BLAH BLAH....YOUR DISREPUTABLE ACQUAINTANCES...BLAH BLAH BLAH... IF YOUR POOR MOTHER KNEW...
"DISREPUTABLE ACQUAINTANCES"? I WOULDN'T SAY THAT!
JANE AVRIL
JANE AVRIL
AND WHO ARE THESE TWO?

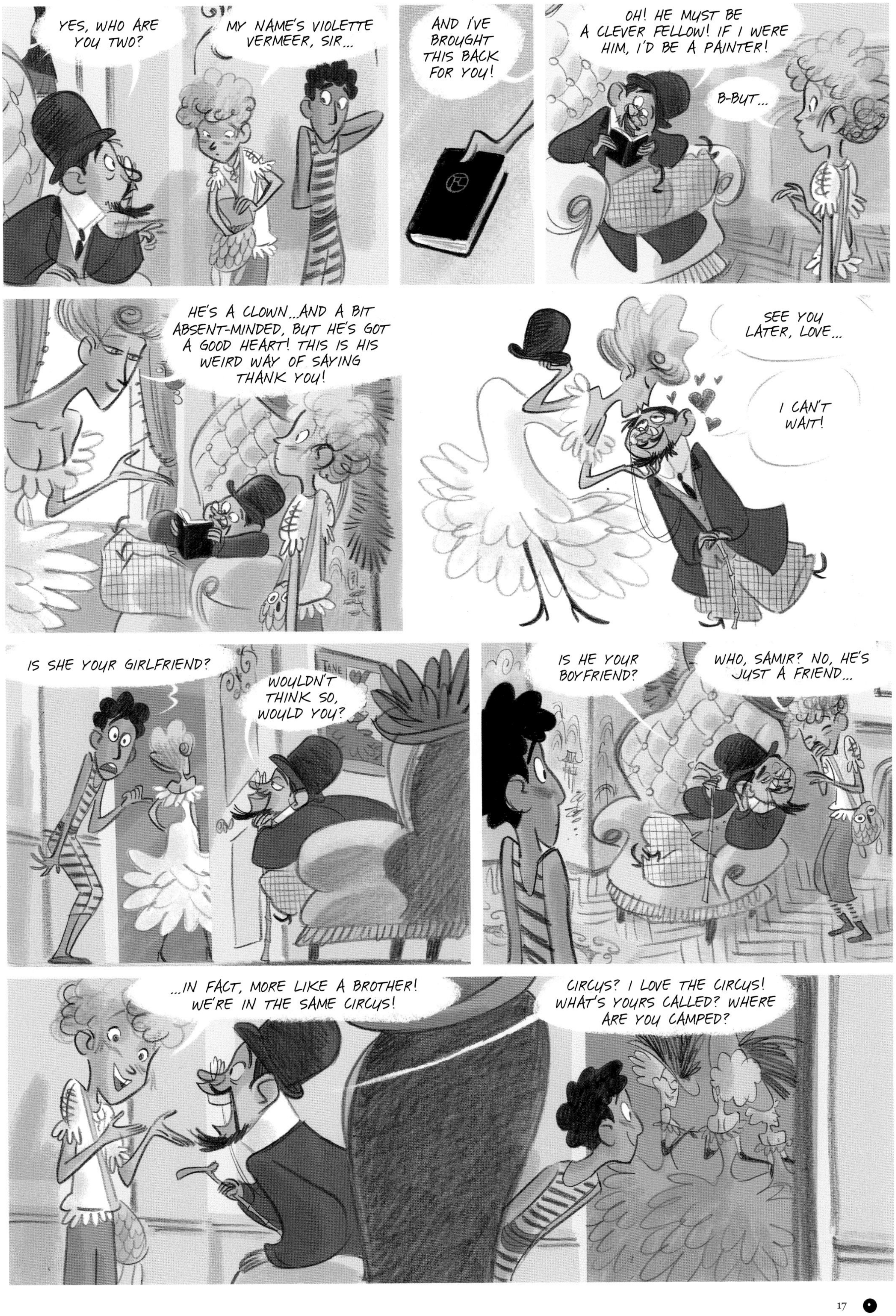
YES, WHO ARE YOU TWO?
MY NAME'S VIOLETTE VERMEER, SIR...
AND I'VE BROUGHT THIS BACK FOR YOU!
OH! HE MUST BE A CLEVER FELLOW! IF I WERE HIM, I'D BE A PAINTER!
B-BUT...
HE'S A CLOWN...AND A BIT ABSENT-MINDED, BUT HE'S GOT A GOOD HEART! THIS IS HIS WEIRD WAY OF SAYING THANK YOU!
SEE YOU LATER, LOVE...
I CAN'T WAIT!
IS SHE YOUR GIRLFRIEND?
WOULDN'T THINK SO, WOULD YOU?
IS HE YOUR BOYFRIEND?
WHO, SAMIR? NO, HE'S JUST A FRIEND...
...IN FACT, MORE LIKE A BROTHER! WE'RE IN THE SAME CIRCUS!
CIRCUS? I LOVE THE CIRCUS! WHAT'S YOURS CALLED? WHERE ARE YOU CAMPED?

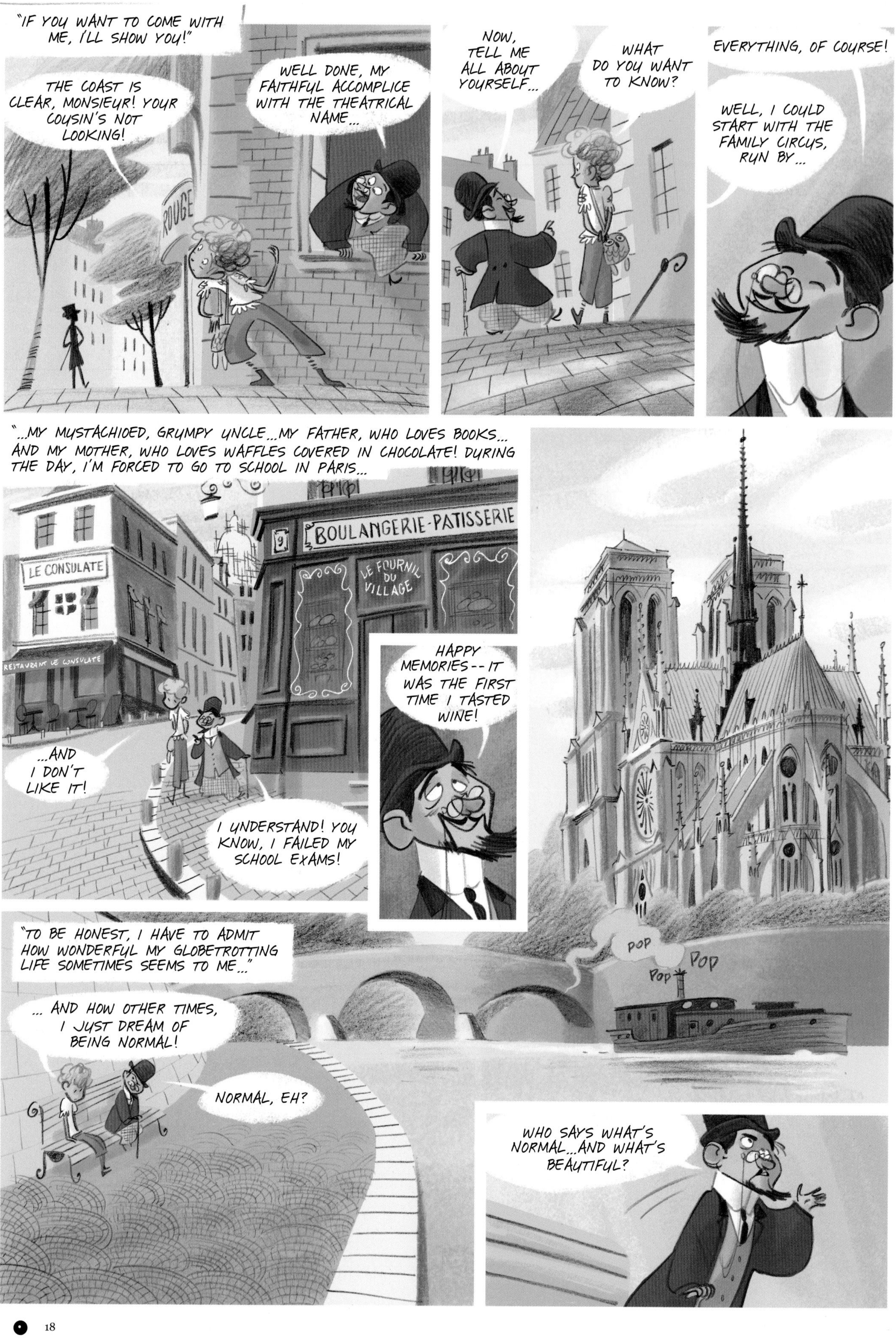
"IF YOU WANT TO COME WITH ME, I'LL SHOW YOU!"
THE COAST IS CLEAR, MONSIEUR! YOUR COUSIN'S NOT LOOKING!
ROUGE
WELL DONE, MY FAITHFUL ACCOMPLICE WITH THE THEATRICAL NAME...
NOW, TELL ME ALL ABOUT YOURSELF...
WHAT DO YOU WANT TO KNOW?
EVERYTHING, OF COURSE!
WELL, I COULD START WITH THE FAMILY CIRCUS, RUN BY...
"...MY MUSTACHIOED, GRUMPY UNCLE...MY FATHER, WHO LOVES BOOKS... AND MY MOTHER, WHO LOVES WAFFLES COVERED IN CHOCOLATE! DURING THE DAY, I'M FORCED TO GO TO SCHOOL IN PARIS...
BOULANGERIE-PATISSERIE
LE FOURNIL DU VILLAGE
LE CONSULATE
RESTAURANT LE CONSULATE
...AND I DON'T LIKE IT!
I UNDERSTAND! YOU KNOW, I FAILED MY SCHOOL EXAMS!
HAPPY MEMORIES -- IT WAS THE FIRST TIME I TASTED WINE!
POP
POP
POP
"TO BE HONEST, I HAVE TO ADMIT HOW WONDERFUL MY GLOBETROTTING LIFE SOMETIMES SEEMS TO ME..."
... AND HOW OTHER TIMES, I JUST DREAM OF BEING NORMAL!
NORMAL, EH?
WHO SAYS WHAT'S NORMAL...AND WHAT'S BEAUTIFUL?

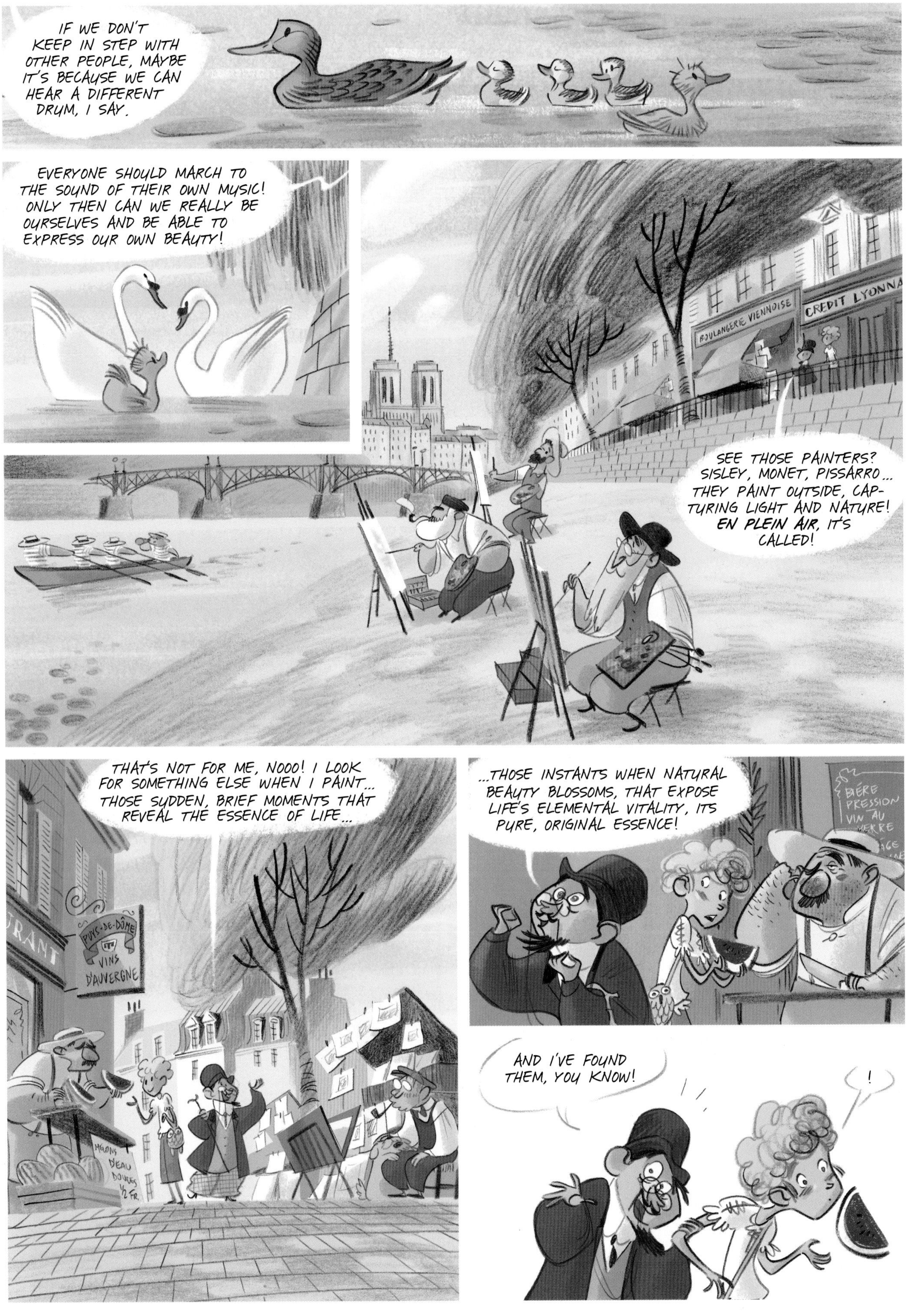
IF WE DON'T KEEP IN STEP WITH OTHER PEOPLE, MAYBE IT'S BECAUSE WE CAN HEAR A DIFFERENT DRUM, I SAY.
EVERYONE SHOULD MARCH TO THE SOUND OF THEIR OWN MUSIC! ONLY THEN CAN WE REALLY BE OURSELVES AND BE ABLE TO EXPRESS OUR OWN BEAUTY!
BOULANGERIE VIENNOISE
CREDIT LYONNA
SEE THOSE PAINTERS? SISLEY, MONET, PISSARRO... THEY PAINT OUTSIDE, CAPTURING LIGHT AND NATURE! EN PLEIN AIR, IT'S CALLED!
THAT'S NOT FOR ME, NOOO! I LOOK FOR SOMETHING ELSE WHEN I PAINT... THOSE SUDDEN, BRIEF MOMENTS THAT REVEAL THE ESSENCE OF LIFE...
PUY-DE-DÔME
VINS D'AUVERGNE
MELONS D'EAU DOUDES 1/2 FR.
...THOSE INSTANTS WHEN NATURAL BEAUTY BLOSSOMS, THAT EXPOSE LIFE'S ELEMENTAL VITALITY, ITS PURE, ORIGINAL ESSENCE!
BIÈRE PRESSION VIN AU VERRE
AND I'VE FOUND THEM, YOU KNOW!
!

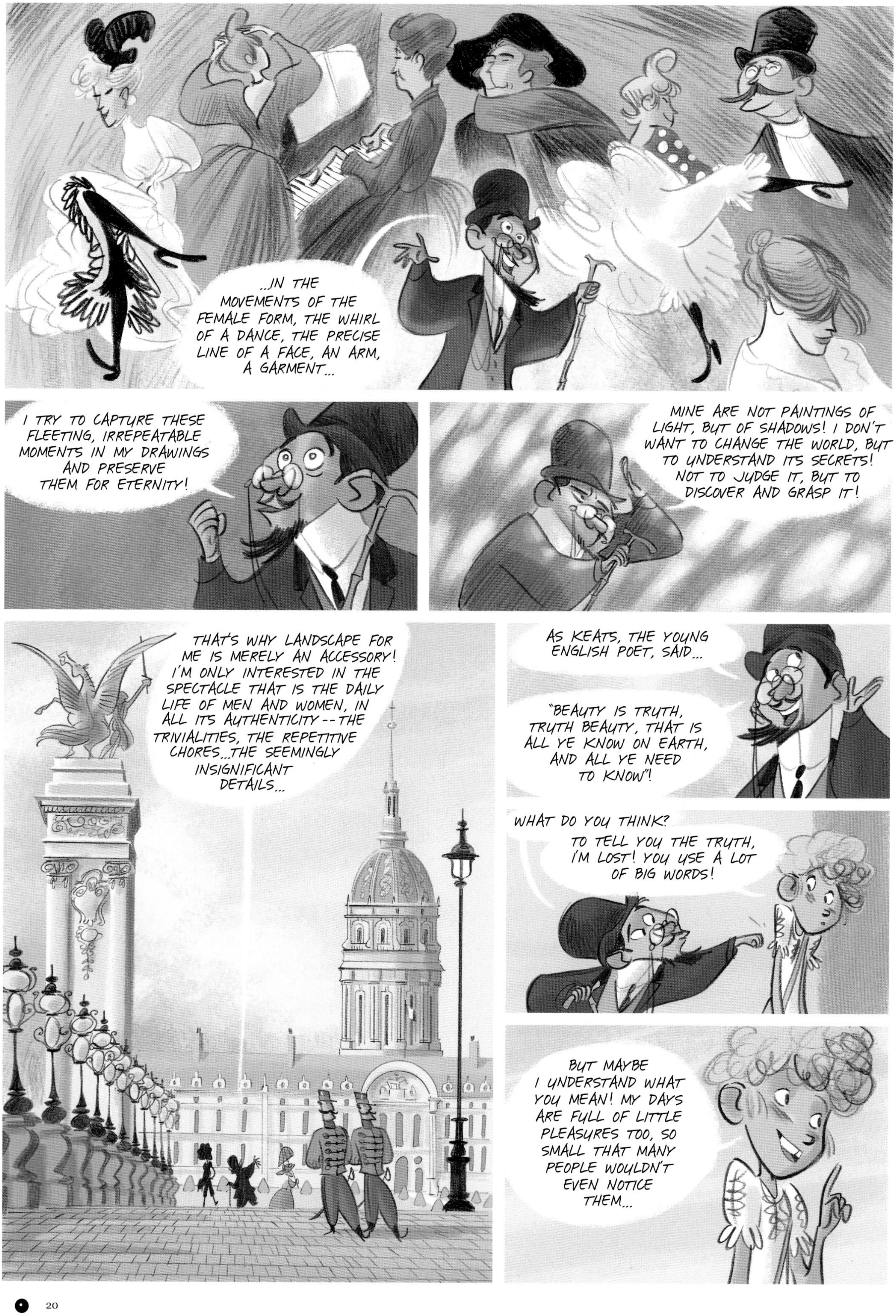
...IN THE MOVEMENTS OF THE FEMALE FORM, THE WHIRL OF A DANCE, THE PRECISE LINE OF A FACE, AN ARM, A GARMENT...
I TRY TO CAPTURE THESE FLEETING, IRREPEATABLE MOMENTS IN MY DRAWINGS AND PRESERVE THEM FOR ETERNITY!
MINE ARE NOT PAINTINGS OF LIGHT, BUT OF SHADOWS! I DON'T WANT TO CHANGE THE WORLD, BUT TO UNDERSTAND ITS SECRETS! NOT TO JUDGE IT, BUT TO DISCOVER AND GRASP IT!
THAT'S WHY LANDSCAPE FOR ME IS MERELY AN ACCESSORY! I'M ONLY INTERESTED IN THE SPECTACLE THAT IS THE DAILY LIFE OF MEN AND WOMEN, IN ALL ITS AUTHENTICITY -- THE TRIVIALITIES, THE REPETITIVE CHORES...THE SEEMINGLY INSIGNIFICANT DETAILS...
AS KEATS, THE YOUNG ENGLISH POET, SAID...
"BEAUTY IS TRUTH, TRUTH BEAUTY, THAT IS ALL YE KNOW ON EARTH, AND ALL YE NEED TO KNOW"!
WHAT DO YOU THINK?
TO TELL YOU THE TRUTH, I'M LOST! YOU USE A LOT OF BIG WORDS!
BUT MAYBE I UNDERSTAND WHAT YOU MEAN! MY DAYS ARE FULL OF LITTLE PLEASURES TOO, SO SMALL THAT MANY PEOPLE WOULDN'T EVEN NOTICE THEM...

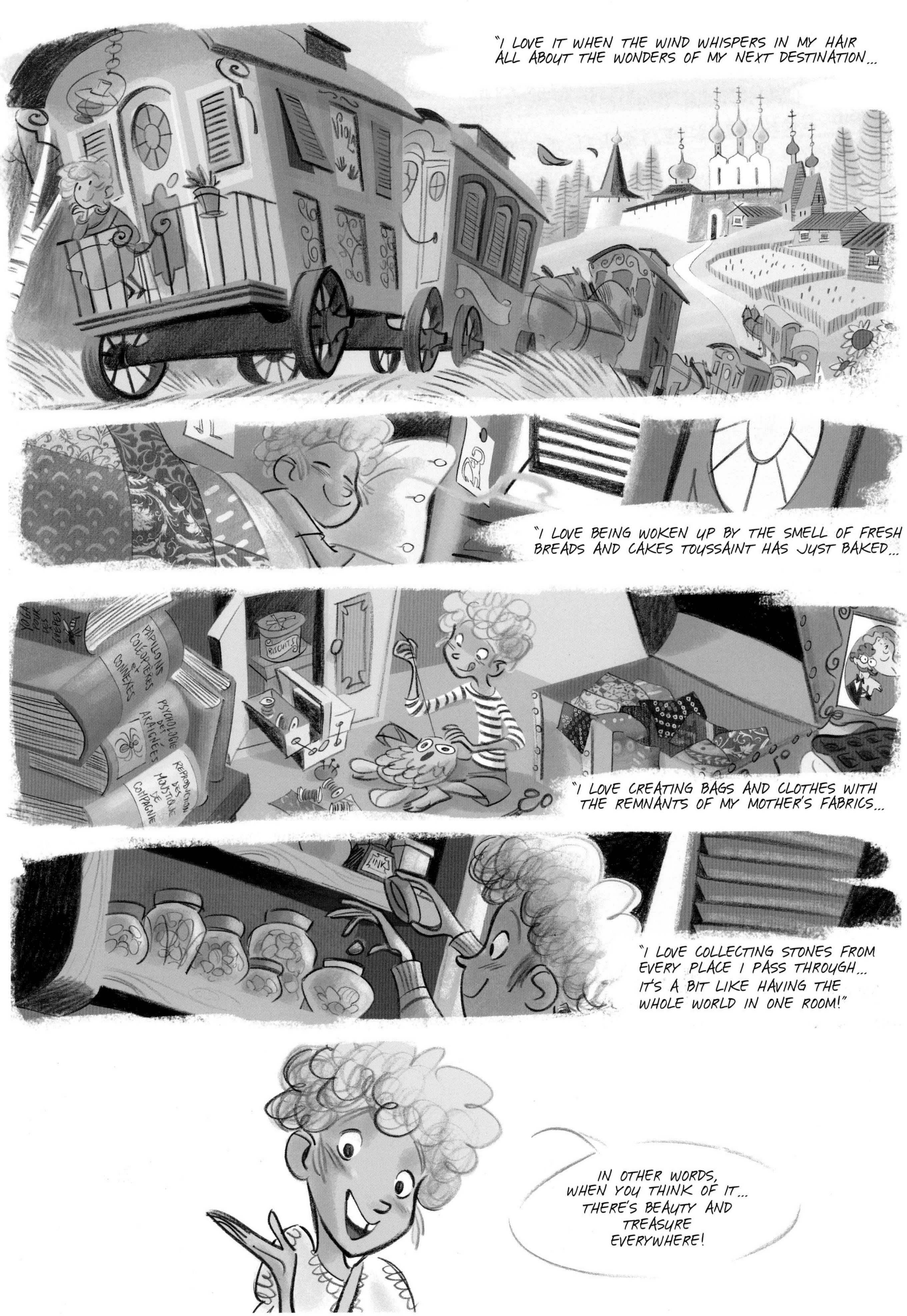
"I LOVE IT WHEN THE WIND WHISPERS IN MY HAIR ALL ABOUT THE WONDERS OF MY NEXT DESTINATION...
"I LOVE BEING WOKEN UP BY THE SMELL OF FRESH BREADS AND CAKES TOUSSAINT HAS JUST BAKED...
"I LOVE CREATING BAGS AND CLOTHES WITH THE REMNANTS OF MY MOTHER'S FABRICS...
"I LOVE COLLECTING STONES FROM EVERY PLACE I PASS THROUGH... IT'S A BIT LIKE HAVING THE WHOLE WORLD IN ONE ROOM!"
IN OTHER WORDS, WHEN YOU THINK OF IT... THERE'S BEAUTY AND TREASURE EVERYWHERE!

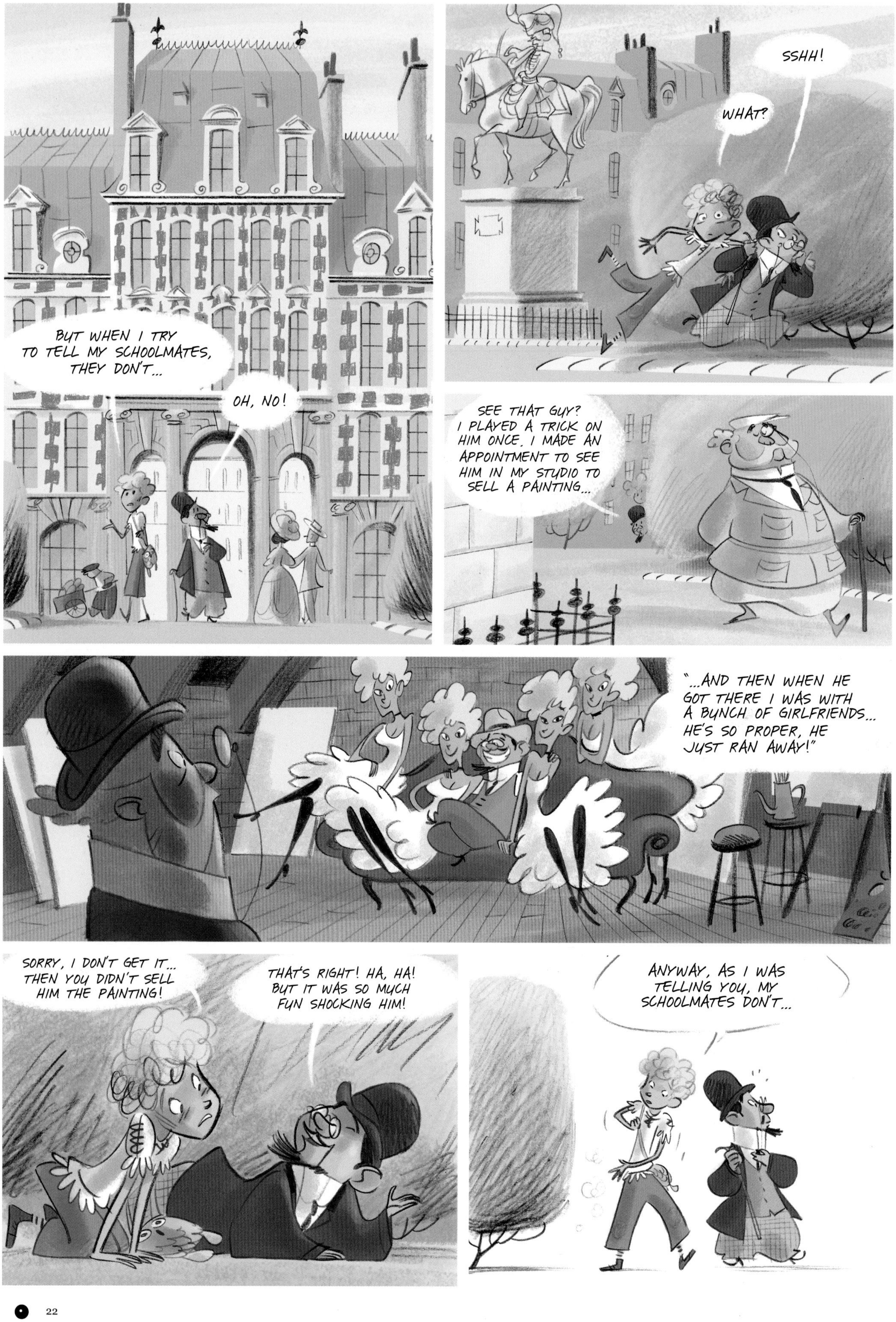
BUT WHEN I TRY TO TELL MY SCHOOLMATES, THEY DON'T...
OH, NO!
WHAT?
SSHH!
SEE THAT GUY? I PLAYED A TRICK ON HIM ONCE. I MADE AN APPOINTMENT TO SEE HIM IN MY STUDIO TO SELL A PAINTING...
"...AND THEN WHEN HE GOT THERE I WAS WITH A BUNCH OF GIRLFRIENDS... HE'S SO PROPER, HE JUST RAN AWAY!"
SORRY, I DON'T GET IT... THEN YOU DIDN'T SELL HIM THE PAINTING!
THAT'S RIGHT! HA, HA! BUT IT WAS SO MUCH FUN SHOCKING HIM!
ANYWAY, AS I WAS TELLING YOU, MY SCHOOLMATES DON'T...

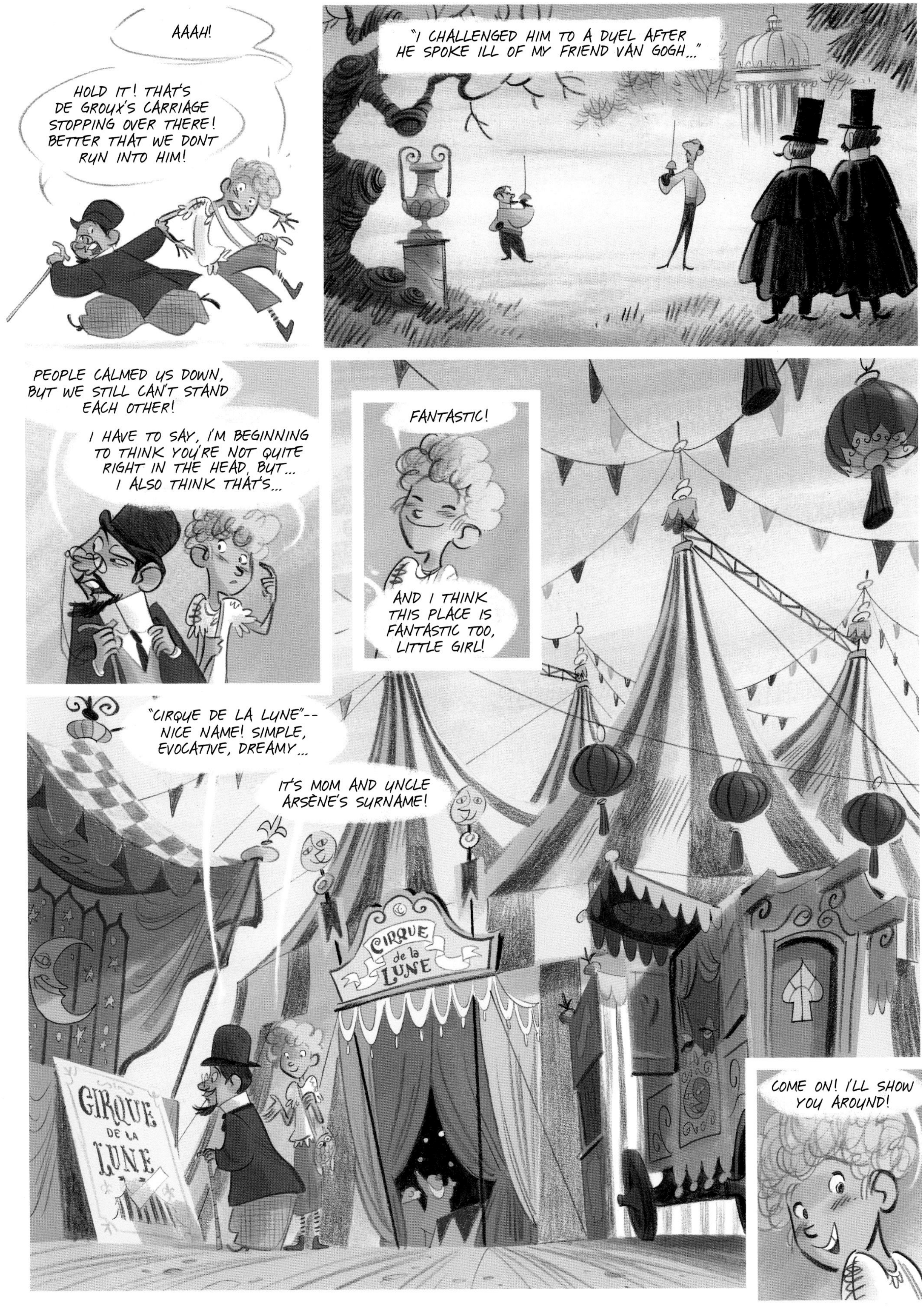
AAAH!
HOLD IT! THAT'S DE GROUX'S CARRIAGE STOPPING OVER THERE! BETTER THAT WE DONT RUN INTO HIM!
"I CHALLENGED HIM TO A DUEL AFTER HE SPOKE ILL OF MY FRIEND VAN GOGH..."
PEOPLE CALMED US DOWN, BUT WE STILL CAN'T STAND EACH OTHER!
I HAVE TO SAY, I'M BEGINNING TO THINK YOU'RE NOT QUITE RIGHT IN THE HEAD, BUT... I ALSO THINK THAT'S...
FANTASTIC!
AND I THINK THIS PLACE IS FANTASTIC TOO, LITTLE GIRL!
"CIRQUE DE LA LUNE"-- NICE NAME! SIMPLE, EVOCATIVE, DREAMY...
IT'S MOM AND UNCLE ARSÈNE'S SURNAME!
CIRQUE de la LUNE
CIRQUE DE LA LUNE
COME ON! I'LL SHOW YOU AROUND!

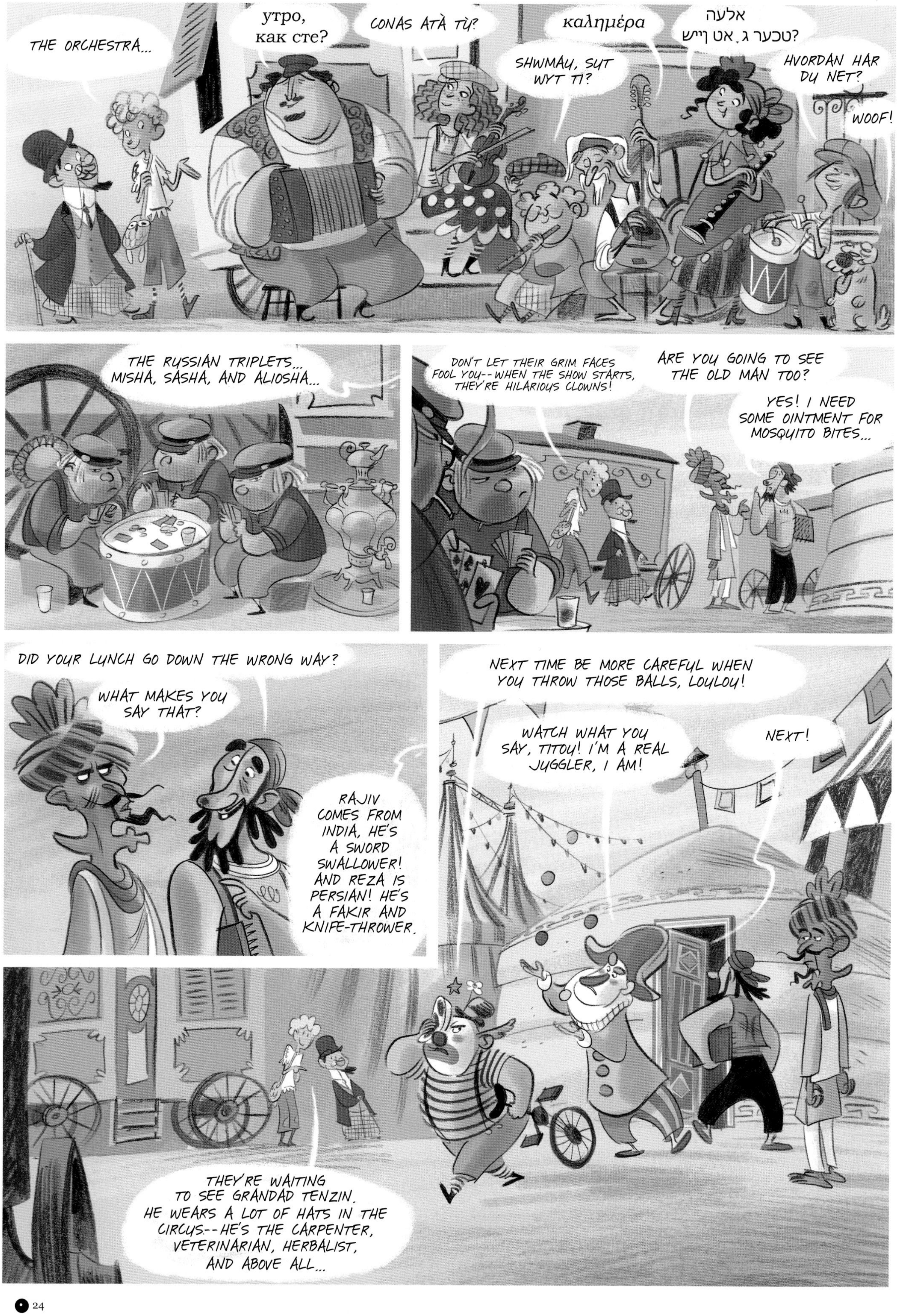
THE ORCHESTRA...
утро,
как сте?
CONAS ATÀ TÙ?
SHWMAU, SUT WYT TI?
καλημέρα
אלעה
טכער ג.אט ווייש?
HVORDAN HAR DU NET?
WOOF!
THE RUSSIAN TRIPLETS... MISHA, SASHA, AND ALIOSHA...
DON'T LET THEIR GRIM FACES FOOL YOU--WHEN THE SHOW STARTS, THEY'RE HILARIOUS CLOWNS!
ARE YOU GOING TO SEE THE OLD MAN TOO?
YES! I NEED SOME OINTMENT FOR MOSQUITO BITES...
DID YOUR LUNCH GO DOWN THE WRONG WAY?
WHAT MAKES YOU SAY THAT?
RAJIV COMES FROM INDIA, HE'S A SWORD SWALLOWER! AND REZA IS PERSIAN! HE'S A FAKIR AND KNIFE-THROWER.
NEXT TIME BE MORE CAREFUL WHEN YOU THROW THOSE BALLS, LOULOU!
WATCH WHAT YOU SAY, TITOU! I'M A REAL JUGGLER, I AM!
NEXT!
THEY'RE WAITING TO SEE GRANDAD TENZIN. HE WEARS A LOT OF HATS IN THE CIRCUS--HE'S THE CARPENTER, VETERINARIAN, HERBALIST, AND ABOVE ALL...

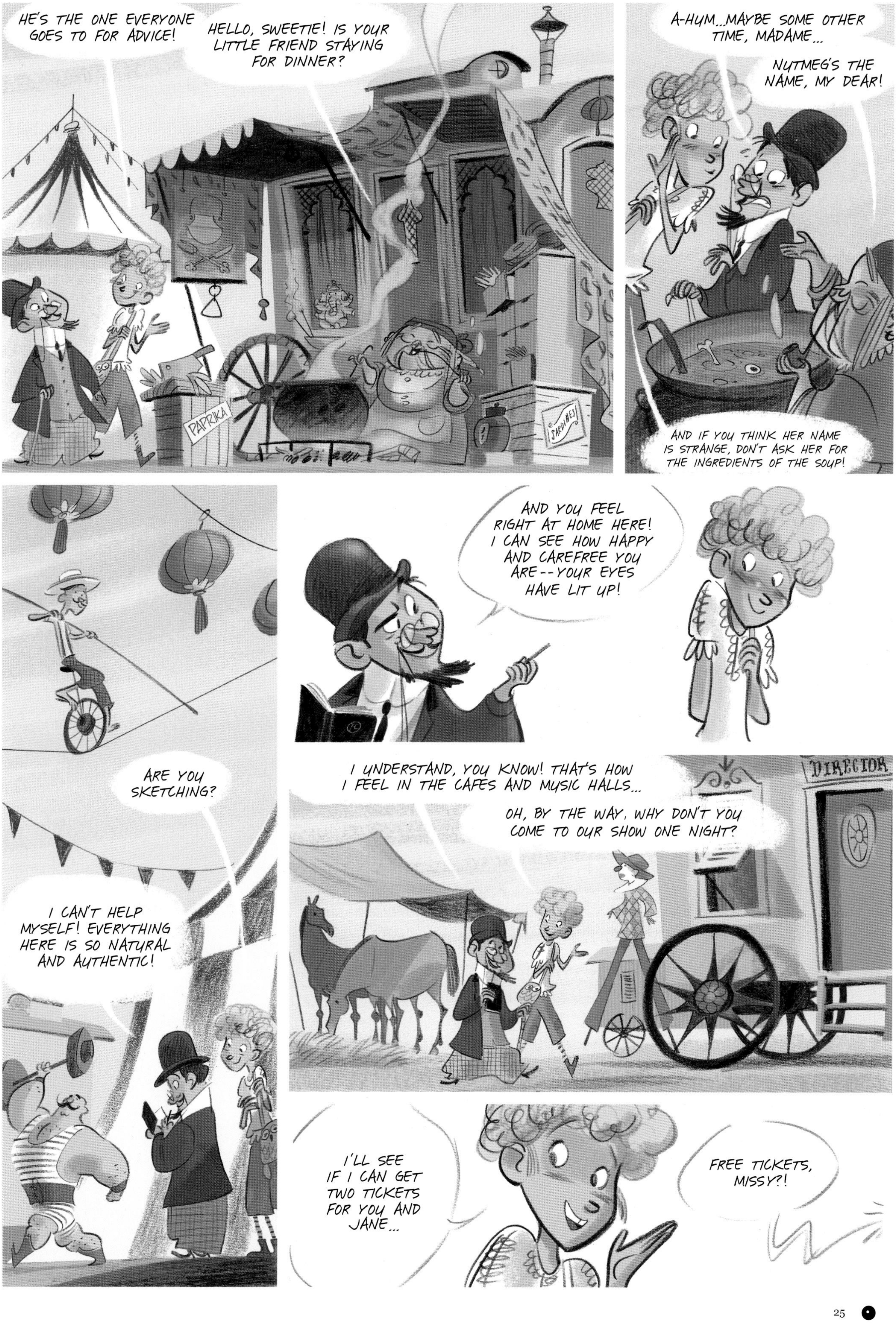
HE'S THE ONE EVERYONE GOES TO FOR ADVICE!
HELLO, SWEETIE! IS YOUR LITTLE FRIEND STAYING FOR DINNER?
PAPRIKA
SARDINES
A-HUM...MAYBE SOME OTHER TIME, MADAME...
NUTMEG'S THE NAME, MY DEAR!
AND IF YOU THINK HER NAME IS STRANGE, DON'T ASK HER FOR THE INGREDIENTS OF THE SOUP!
AND YOU FEEL RIGHT AT HOME HERE! I CAN SEE HOW HAPPY AND CAREFREE YOU ARE--YOUR EYES HAVE LIT UP!
ARE YOU SKETCHING?
I CAN'T HELP MYSELF! EVERYTHING HERE IS SO NATURAL AND AUTHENTIC!
I UNDERSTAND, YOU KNOW! THAT'S HOW I FEEL IN THE CAFES AND MUSIC HALLS...
OH, BY THE WAY, WHY DON'T YOU COME TO OUR SHOW ONE NIGHT?
DIRECTOR
I'LL SEE IF I CAN GET TWO TICKETS FOR YOU AND JANE...
FREE TICKETS, MISSY?!

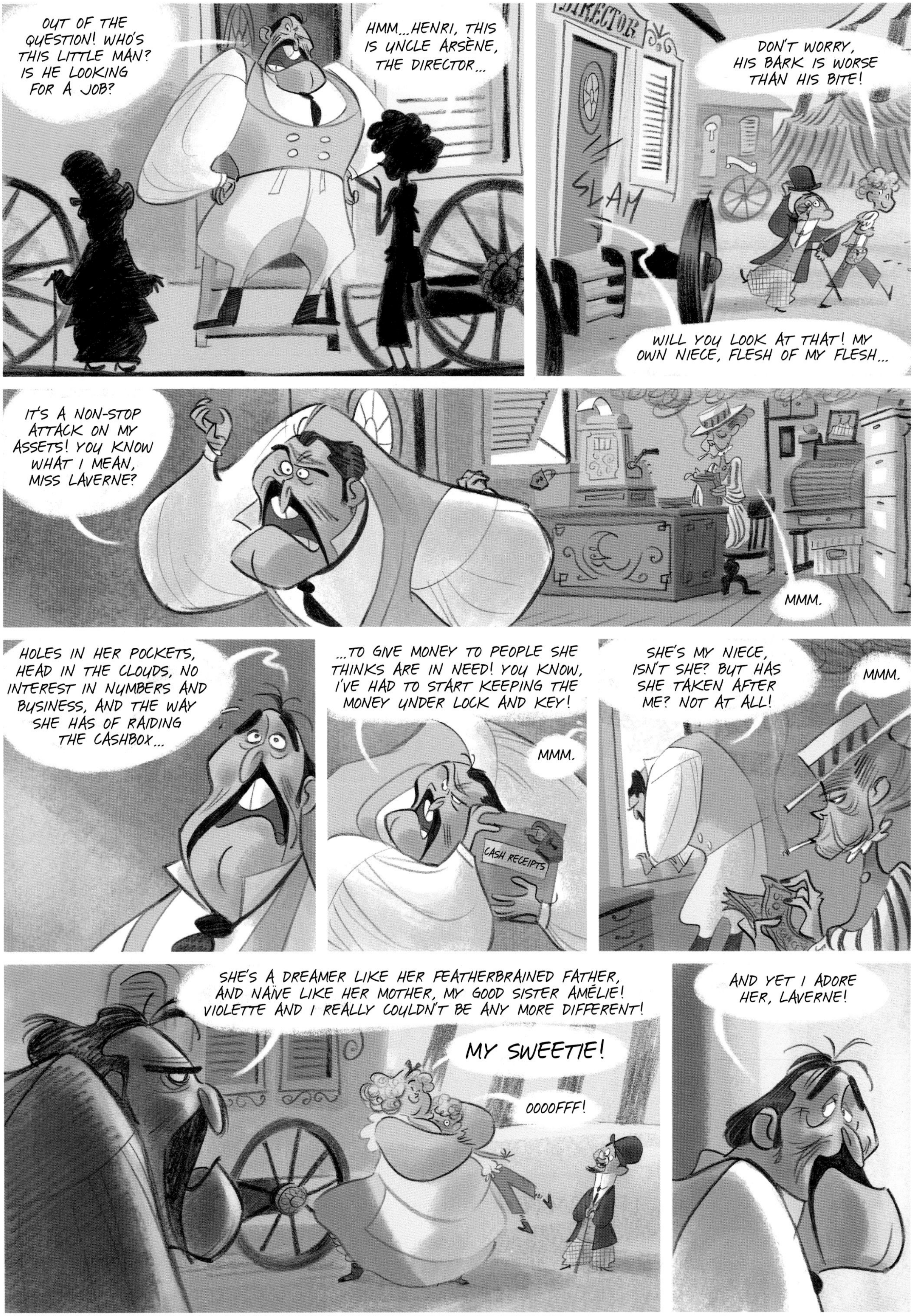
OUT OF THE QUESTION! WHO'S THIS LITTLE MAN? IS HE LOOKING FOR A JOB?
HMM... HENRI, THIS IS UNCLE ARSÈNE, THE DIRECTOR...
DIRECTOR
SLAM
DON'T WORRY, HIS BARK IS WORSE THAN HIS BITE!
WILL YOU LOOK AT THAT! MY OWN NIECE, FLESH OF MY FLESH...
IT'S A NON-STOP ATTACK ON MY ASSETS! YOU KNOW WHAT I MEAN, MISS LAVERNE?
MMM.
HOLES IN HER POCKETS, HEAD IN THE CLOUDS, NO INTEREST IN NUMBERS AND BUSINESS, AND THE WAY SHE HAS OF RAIDING THE CASHBOX...
...TO GIVE MONEY TO PEOPLE SHE THINKS ARE IN NEED! YOU KNOW, I'VE HAD TO START KEEPING THE MONEY UNDER LOCK AND KEY!
MMM.
CASH RECEIPTS
SHE'S MY NIECE, ISN'T SHE? BUT HAS SHE TAKEN AFTER ME? NOT AT ALL!
MMM.
SHE'S A DREAMER LIKE HER FEATHERBRAINED FATHER, AND NAÏVE LIKE HER MOTHER, MY GOOD SISTER AMÉLIE! VIOLETTE AND I REALLY COULDN'T BE ANY MORE DIFFERENT!
MY SWEETIE!
OOOOFFF!
AND YET I ADORE HER, LAVERNE!

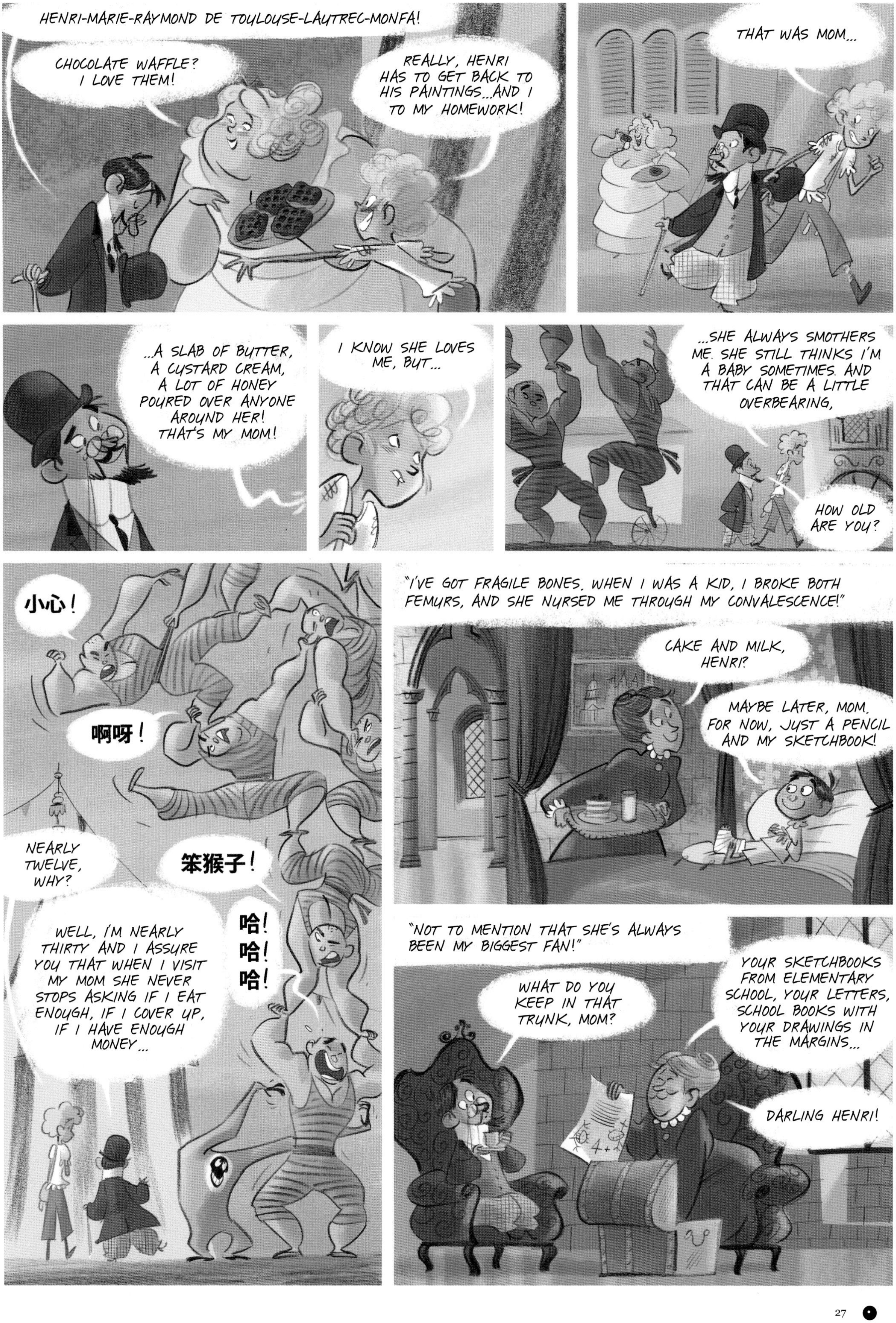
HENRI-MARIE-RAYMOND DE TOULOUSE-LAUTREC-MONFA!
CHOCOLATE WAFFLE? I LOVE THEM!
REALLY, HENRI HAS TO GET BACK TO HIS PAINTINGS...AND I TO MY HOMEWORK!
THAT WAS MOM...
...A SLAB OF BUTTER, A CUSTARD CREAM, A LOT OF HONEY POURED OVER ANYONE AROUND HER! THAT'S MY MOM!
I KNOW SHE LOVES ME, BUT...
...SHE ALWAYS SMOTHERS ME. SHE STILL THINKS I'M A BABY SOMETIMES. AND THAT CAN BE A LITTLE OVERBEARING.
HOW OLD ARE YOU?
小心！
啊呀！
NEARLY TWELVE, WHY?
笨猴子！
哈！哈！哈！
WELL, I'M NEARLY THIRTY AND I ASSURE YOU THAT WHEN I VISIT MY MOM SHE NEVER STOPS ASKING IF I EAT ENOUGH, IF I COVER UP, IF I HAVE ENOUGH MONEY...
"I'VE GOT FRAGILE BONES. WHEN I WAS A KID, I BROKE BOTH FEMURS, AND SHE NURSED ME THROUGH MY CONVALESCENCE!"
CAKE AND MILK, HENRI?
MAYBE LATER, MOM. FOR NOW, JUST A PENCIL AND MY SKETCHBOOK!
"NOT TO MENTION THAT SHE'S ALWAYS BEEN MY BIGGEST FAN!"
WHAT DO YOU KEEP IN THAT TRUNK, MOM?
YOUR SKETCHBOOKS FROM ELEMENTARY SCHOOL, YOUR LETTERS, SCHOOL BOOKS WITH YOUR DRAWINGS IN THE MARGINS...
DARLING HENRI!

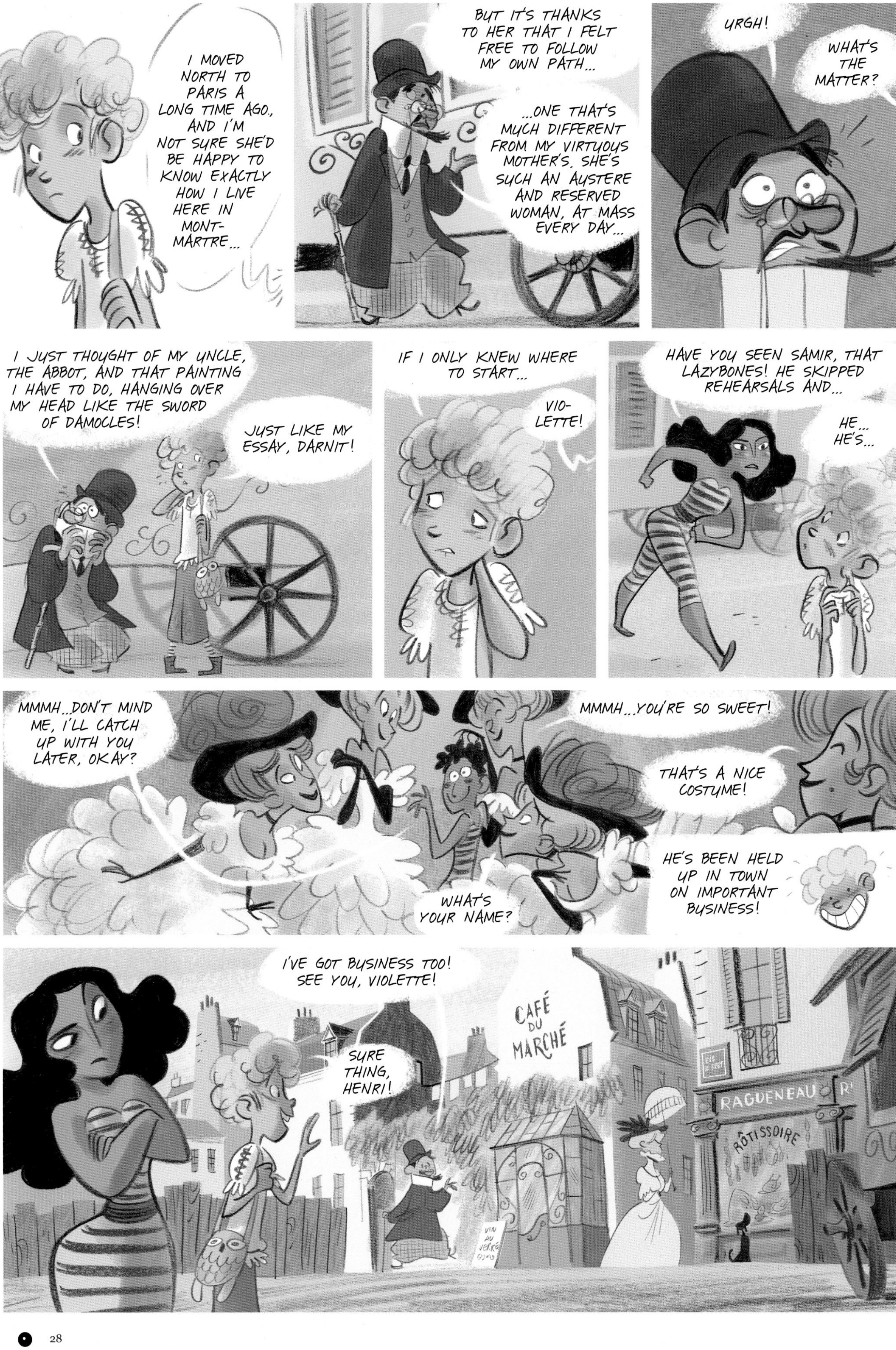
I MOVED NORTH TO PARIS A LONG TIME AGO, AND I'M NOT SURE SHE'D BE HAPPY TO KNOW EXACTLY HOW I LIVE HERE IN MONT-MARTRE...
BUT IT'S THANKS TO HER THAT I FELT FREE TO FOLLOW MY OWN PATH...
...ONE THAT'S MUCH DIFFERENT FROM MY VIRTUOUS MOTHER'S. SHE'S SUCH AN AUSTERE AND RESERVED WOMAN, AT MASS EVERY DAY...
URGH!
WHAT'S THE MATTER?
I JUST THOUGHT OF MY UNCLE, THE ABBOT, AND THAT PAINTING I HAVE TO DO, HANGING OVER MY HEAD LIKE THE SWORD OF DAMOCLES!
JUST LIKE MY ESSAY, DARNIT!
IF I ONLY KNEW WHERE TO START...
VIO-LETTE!
HAVE YOU SEEN SAMIR, THAT LAZYBONES! HE SKIPPED REHEARSALS AND...
HE... HE'S...
MMMH...DON'T MIND ME, I'LL CATCH UP WITH YOU LATER, OKAY?
MMMH...YOU'RE SO SWEET!
THAT'S A NICE COSTUME!
WHAT'S YOUR NAME?
HE'S BEEN HELD UP IN TOWN ON IMPORTANT BUSINESS!
I'VE GOT BUSINESS TOO! SEE YOU, VIOLETTE!
SURE THING, HENRI!
CAFÉ DU MARCHÉ
RAGUENEAU
RÔTISSOIRE
VIN DU VERRE

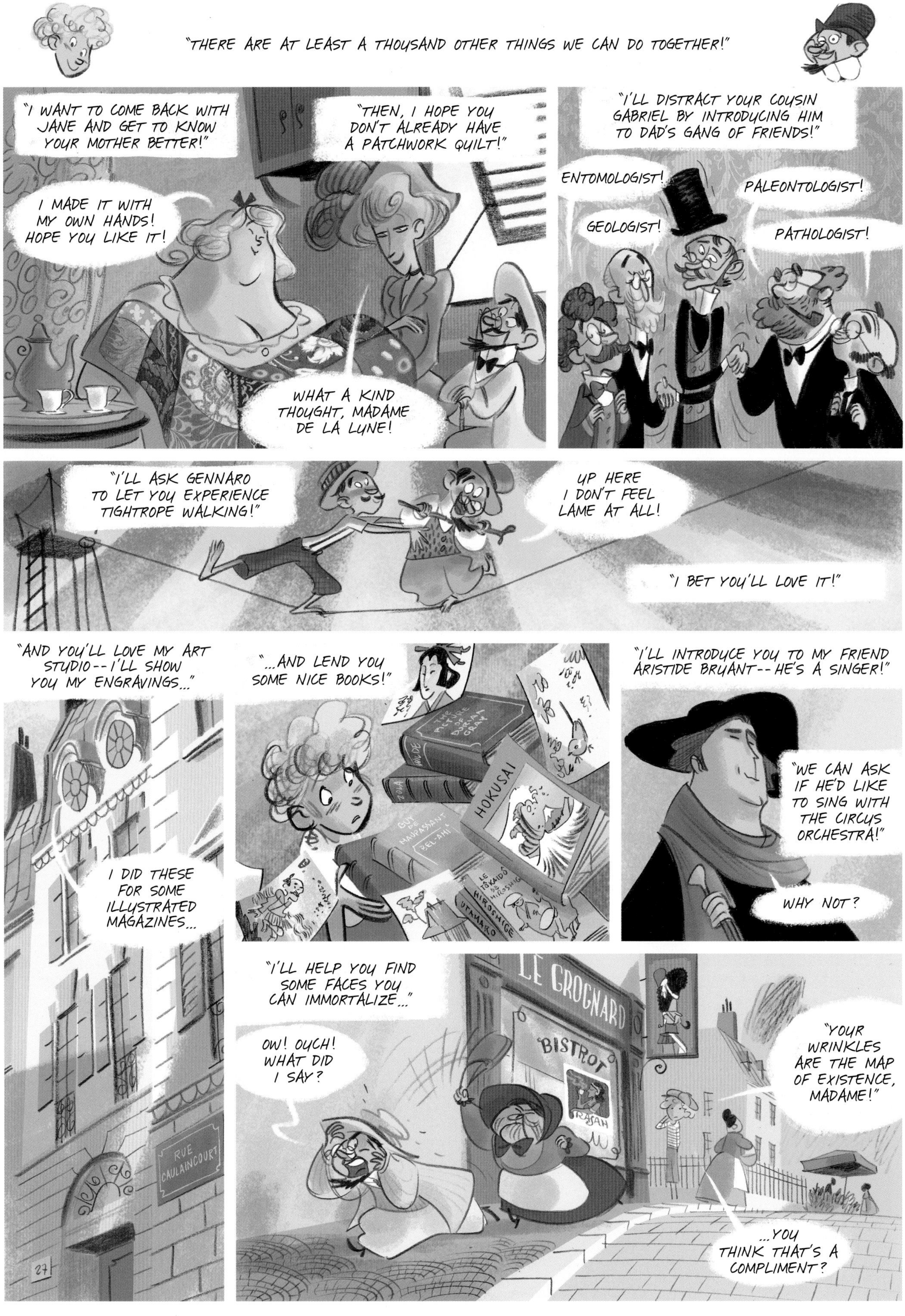
"THERE ARE AT LEAST A THOUSAND OTHER THINGS WE CAN DO TOGETHER!"
"I WANT TO COME BACK WITH JANE AND GET TO KNOW YOUR MOTHER BETTER!"
"THEN, I HOPE YOU DON'T ALREADY HAVE A PATCHWORK QUILT!"
I MADE IT WITH MY OWN HANDS! HOPE YOU LIKE IT!
WHAT A KIND THOUGHT, MADAME DE LA LUNE!
"I'LL DISTRACT YOUR COUSIN GABRIEL BY INTRODUCING HIM TO DAD'S GANG OF FRIENDS!"
ENTOMOLOGIST!
GEOLOGIST!
PALEONTOLOGIST!
PATHOLOGIST!
"I'LL ASK GENNARO TO LET YOU EXPERIENCE TIGHTROPE WALKING!"
UP HERE I DON'T FEEL LAME AT ALL!
"I BET YOU'LL LOVE IT!"
"AND YOU'LL LOVE MY ART STUDIO--I'LL SHOW YOU MY ENGRAVINGS..."
I DID THESE FOR SOME ILLUSTRATED MAGAZINES...
RUE CAULAINCOURT
27
"...AND LEND YOU SOME NICE BOOKS!"
THE PICTURE OF DORIAN GRAY
WILDE
ZOLA
HOKUSAI
GUY DE MAUPASSANT
BEL-AMI
HIROSHIGE
UTAMARO
"I'LL INTRODUCE YOU TO MY FRIEND ARISTIDE BRUANT--HE'S A SINGER!"
"WE CAN ASK IF HE'D LIKE TO SING WITH THE CIRCUS ORCHESTRA!"
WHY NOT?
"I'LL HELP YOU FIND SOME FACES YOU CAN IMMORTALIZE..."
LE GROGNARD
BISTROT
OW! OUCH! WHAT DID I SAY?
"YOUR WRINKLES ARE THE MAP OF EXISTENCE, MADAME!"
...YOU THINK THAT'S A COMPLIMENT?

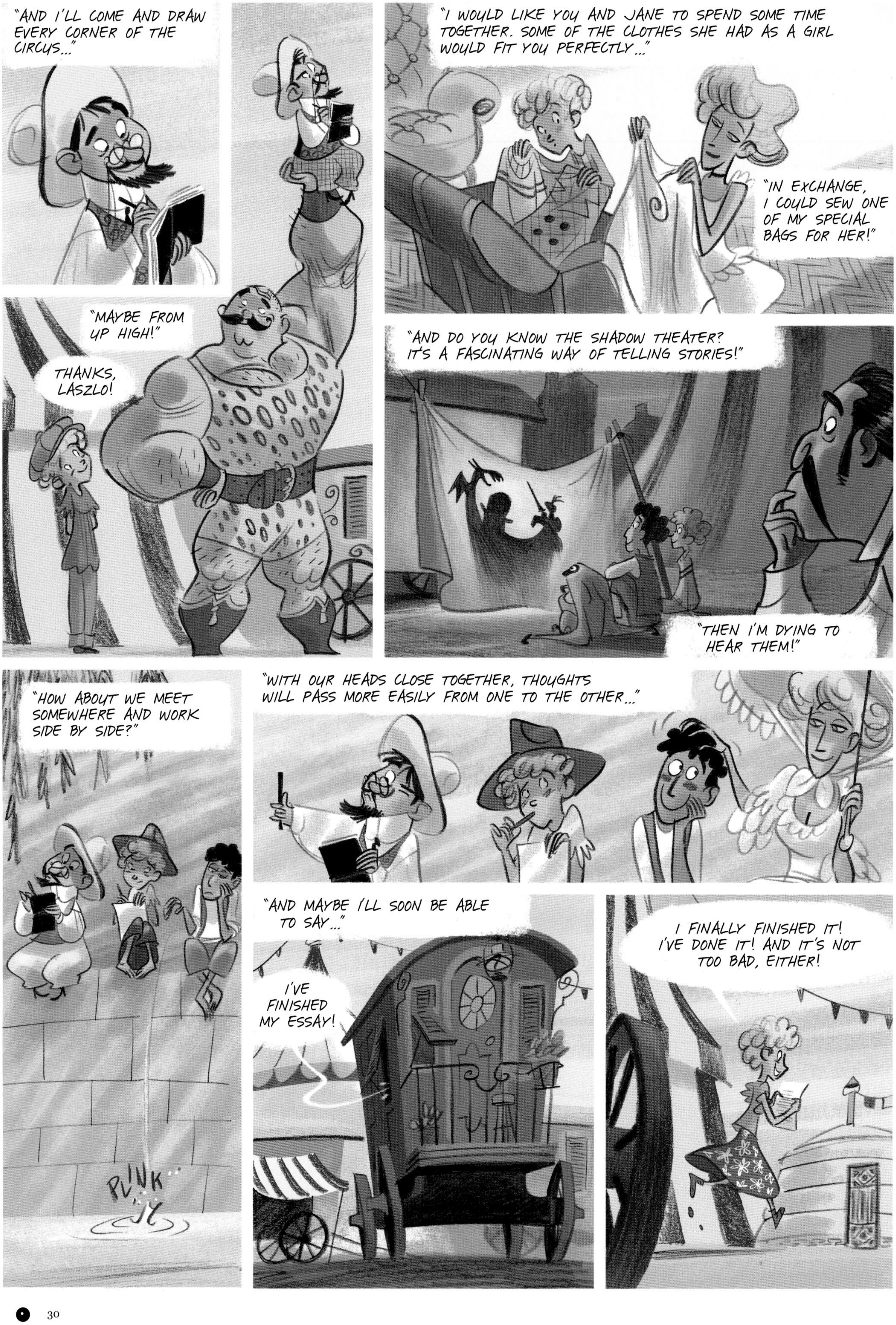
"AND I'LL COME AND DRAW EVERY CORNER OF THE CIRCUS..."
"I WOULD LIKE YOU AND JANE TO SPEND SOME TIME TOGETHER. SOME OF THE CLOTHES SHE HAD AS A GIRL WOULD FIT YOU PERFECTLY..."
"IN EXCHANGE, I COULD SEW ONE OF MY SPECIAL BAGS FOR HER!"
"MAYBE FROM UP HIGH!"
THANKS, LASZLO!
"AND DO YOU KNOW THE SHADOW THEATER? IT'S A FASCINATING WAY OF TELLING STORIES!"
"THEN I'M DYING TO HEAR THEM!"
"HOW ABOUT WE MEET SOMEWHERE AND WORK SIDE BY SIDE?"
PLINK...
"WITH OUR HEADS CLOSE TOGETHER, THOUGHTS WILL PASS MORE EASILY FROM ONE TO THE OTHER..."
"AND MAYBE I'LL SOON BE ABLE TO SAY..."
I'VE FINISHED MY ESSAY!
I FINALLY FINISHED IT! I'VE DONE IT! AND IT'S NOT TOO BAD, EITHER!

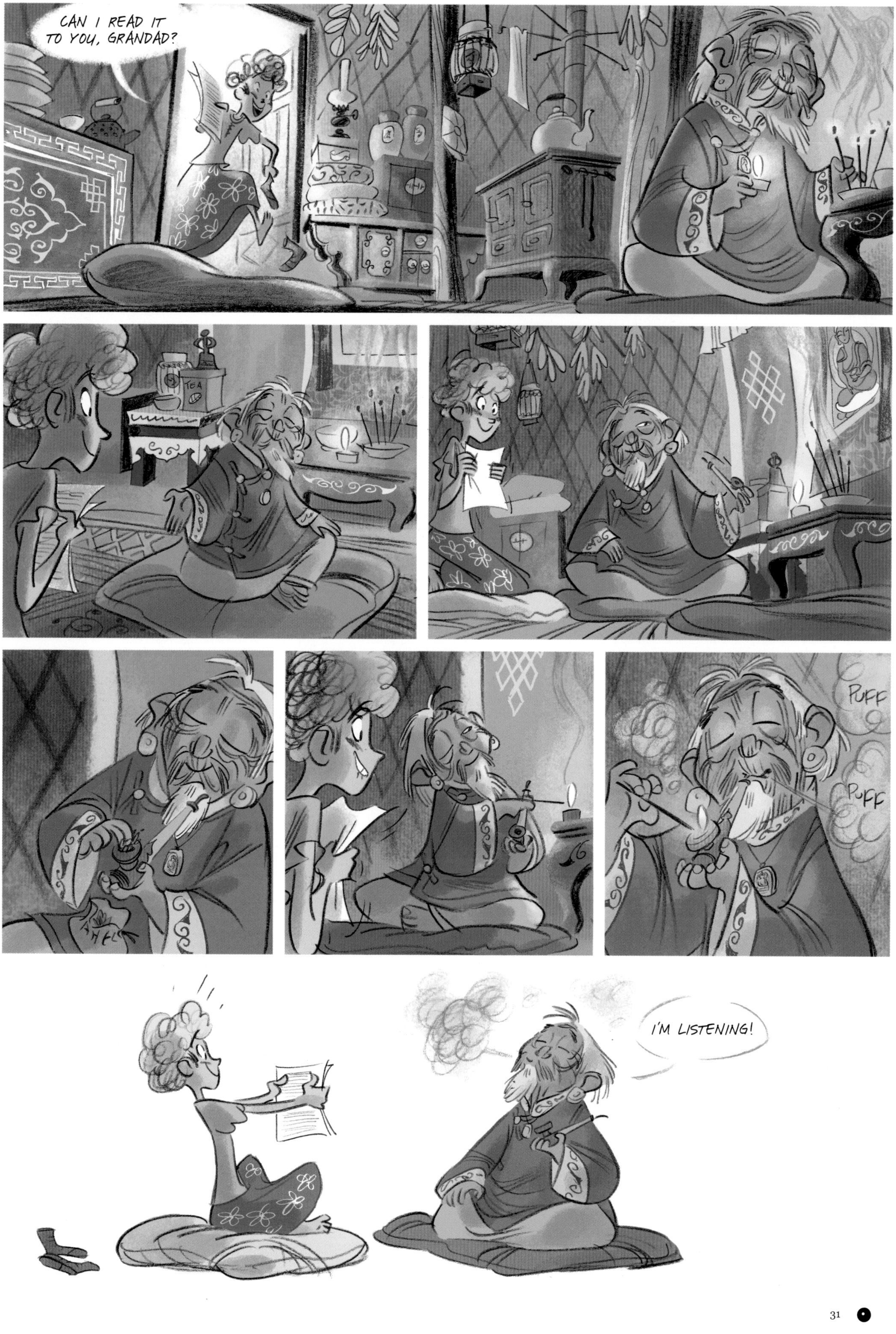
CAN I READ IT TO YOU, GRANDAD?
TEA
PUFF
PUFF
I'M LISTENING!

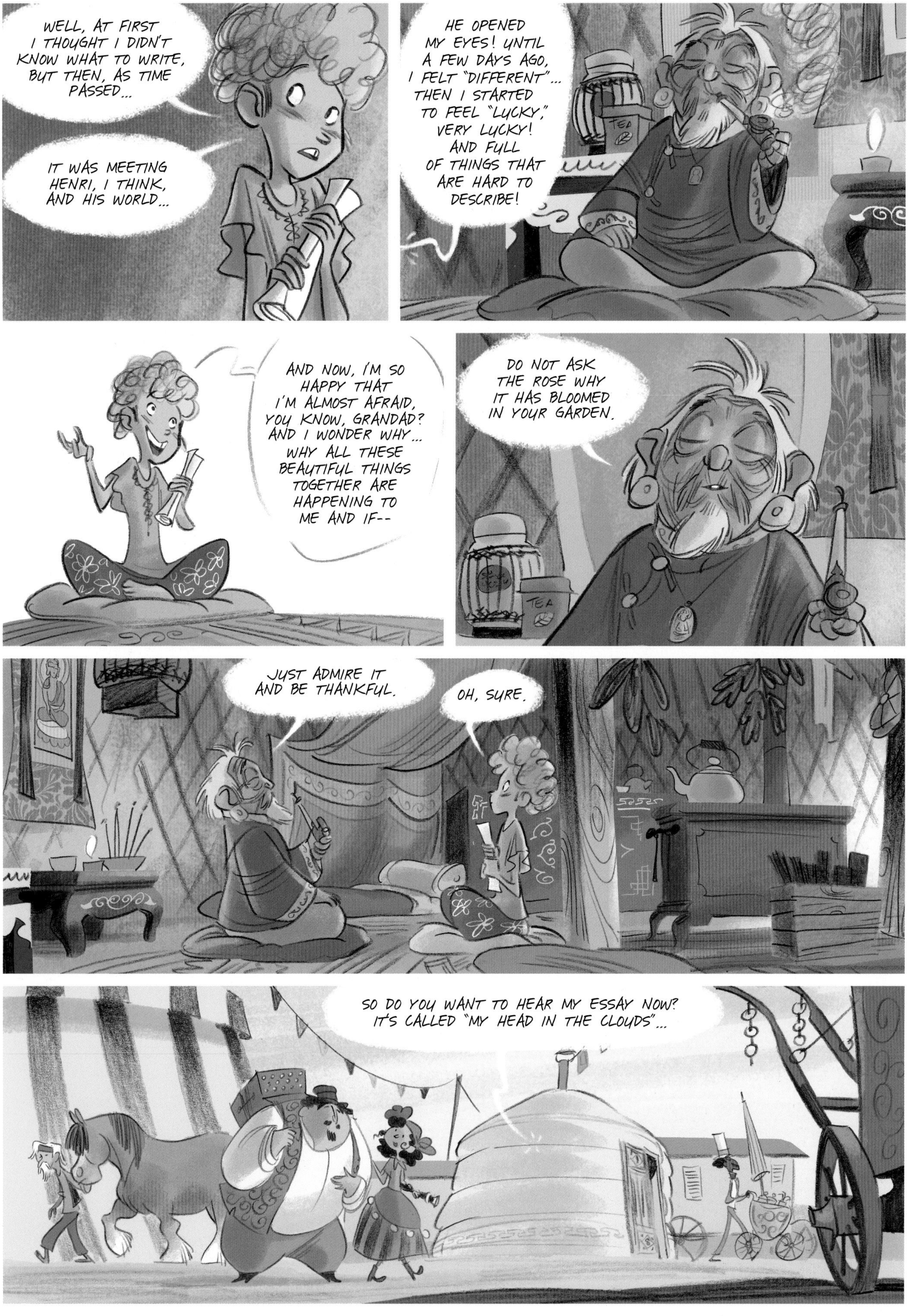
WELL, AT FIRST I THOUGHT I DIDN'T KNOW WHAT TO WRITE, BUT THEN, AS TIME PASSED...
IT WAS MEETING HENRI, I THINK, AND HIS WORLD...
HE OPENED MY EYES! UNTIL A FEW DAYS AGO, I FELT "DIFFERENT"... THEN I STARTED TO FEEL "LUCKY," VERY LUCKY! AND FULL OF THINGS THAT ARE HARD TO DESCRIBE!
TEA
AND NOW, I'M SO HAPPY THAT I'M ALMOST AFRAID, YOU KNOW, GRANDAD? AND I WONDER WHY... WHY ALL THESE BEAUTIFUL THINGS TOGETHER ARE HAPPENING TO ME AND IF--
DO NOT ASK THE ROSE WHY IT HAS BLOOMED IN YOUR GARDEN.
TEA
JUST ADMIRE IT AND BE THANKFUL.
OH, SURE.
SO DO YOU WANT TO HEAR MY ESSAY NOW? IT'S CALLED "MY HEAD IN THE CLOUDS"...

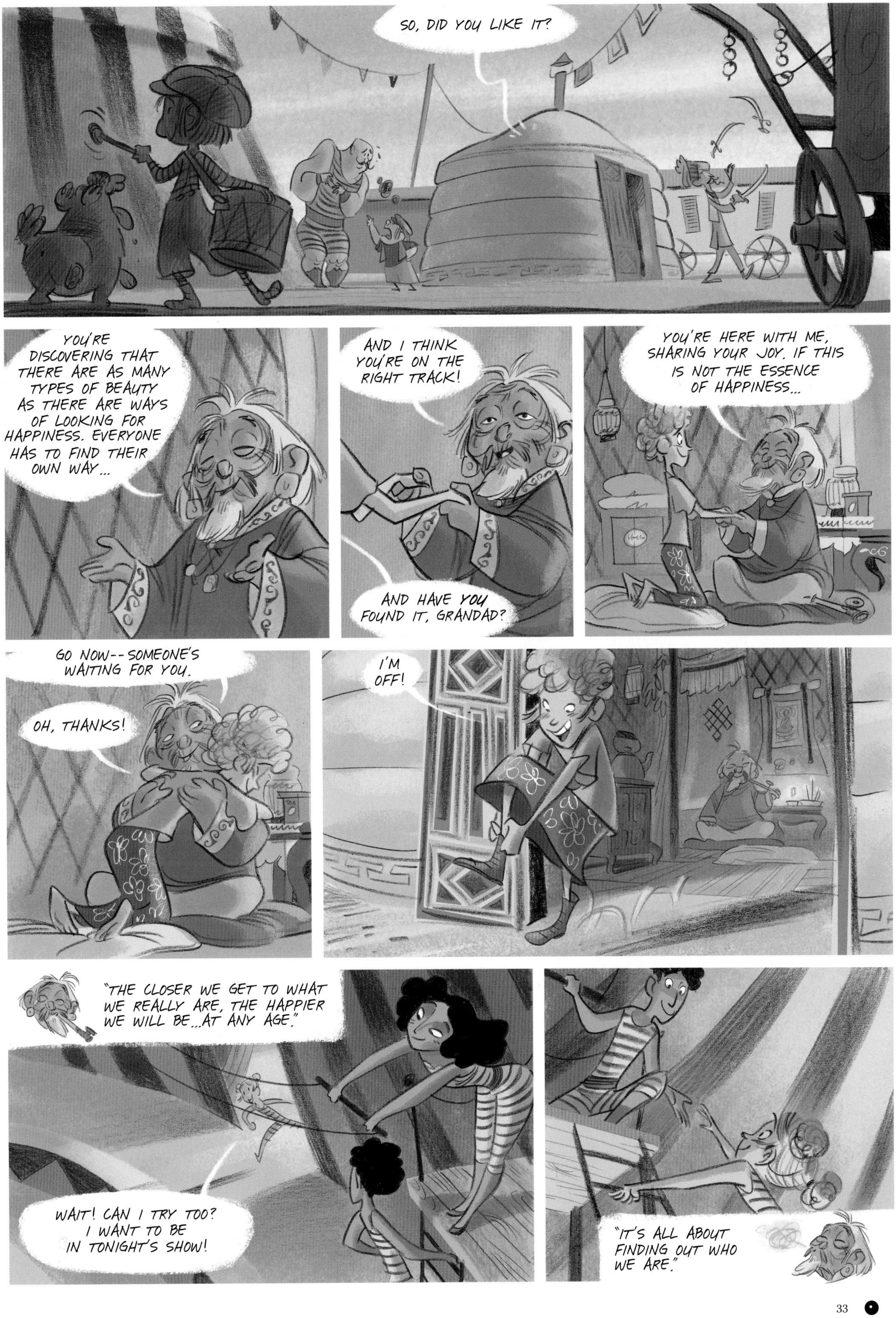

SO, DID YOU LIKE IT?
YOU'RE DISCOVERING THAT THERE ARE AS MANY TYPES OF BEAUTY AS THERE ARE WAYS OF LOOKING FOR HAPPINESS. EVERYONE HAS TO FIND THEIR OWN WAY...
AND I THINK YOU'RE ON THE RIGHT TRACK!
AND HAVE YOU FOUND IT, GRANDAD?
YOU'RE HERE WITH ME, SHARING YOUR JOY. IF THIS IS NOT THE ESSENCE OF HAPPINESS...
GO NOW--SOMEONE'S WAITING FOR YOU.
OH, THANKS!
I'M OFF!
"THE CLOSER WE GET TO WHAT WE REALLY ARE, THE HAPPIER WE WILL BE...AT ANY AGE."
WAIT! CAN I TRY TOO? I WANT TO BE IN TONIGHT'S SHOW!
"IT'S ALL ABOUT FINDING OUT WHO WE ARE."

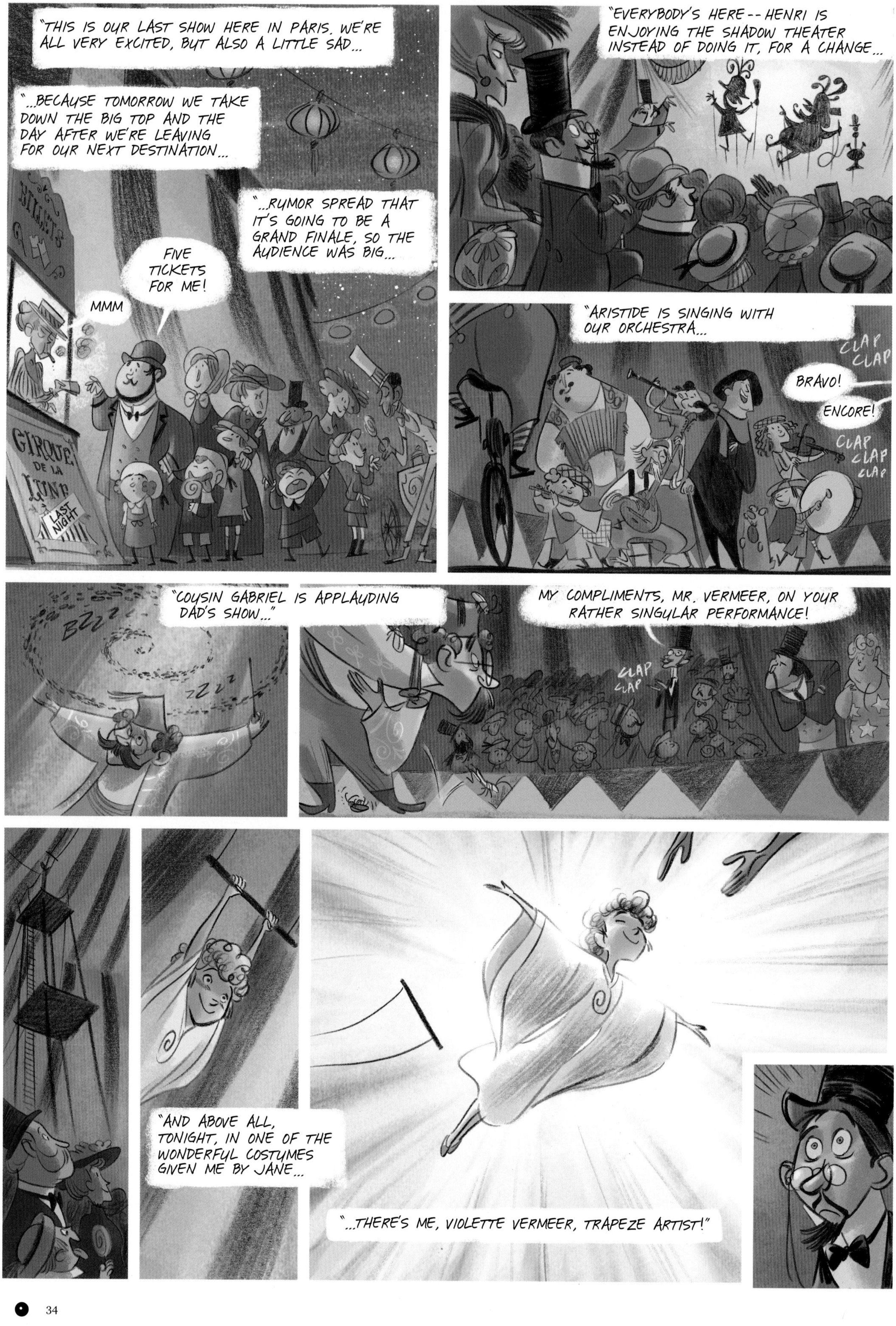
"THIS IS OUR LAST SHOW HERE IN PARIS. WE'RE ALL VERY EXCITED, BUT ALSO A LITTLE SAD...
"...BECAUSE TOMORROW WE TAKE DOWN THE BIG TOP AND THE DAY AFTER WE'RE LEAVING FOR OUR NEXT DESTINATION...
"...RUMOR SPREAD THAT IT'S GOING TO BE A GRAND FINALE, SO THE AUDIENCE WAS BIG...
FIVE TICKETS FOR ME!
MMM
CIRQUE DE LA LUNE
LAST NIGHT
"EVERYBODY'S HERE-- HENRI IS ENJOYING THE SHADOW THEATER INSTEAD OF DOING IT, FOR A CHANGE...
"ARISTIDE IS SINGING WITH OUR ORCHESTRA...
CLAP CLAP
BRAVO!
ENCORE!
CLAP CLAP CLAP
"COUSIN GABRIEL IS APPLAUDING DAD'S SHOW..."
BZZZZ
ZZZZ
MY COMPLIMENTS, MR. VERMEER, ON YOUR RATHER SINGULAR PERFORMANCE!
CLAP CLAP
"AND ABOVE ALL, TONIGHT, IN ONE OF THE WONDERFUL COSTUMES GIVEN ME BY JANE...
"...THERE'S ME, VIOLETTE VERMEER, TRAPEZE ARTIST!"

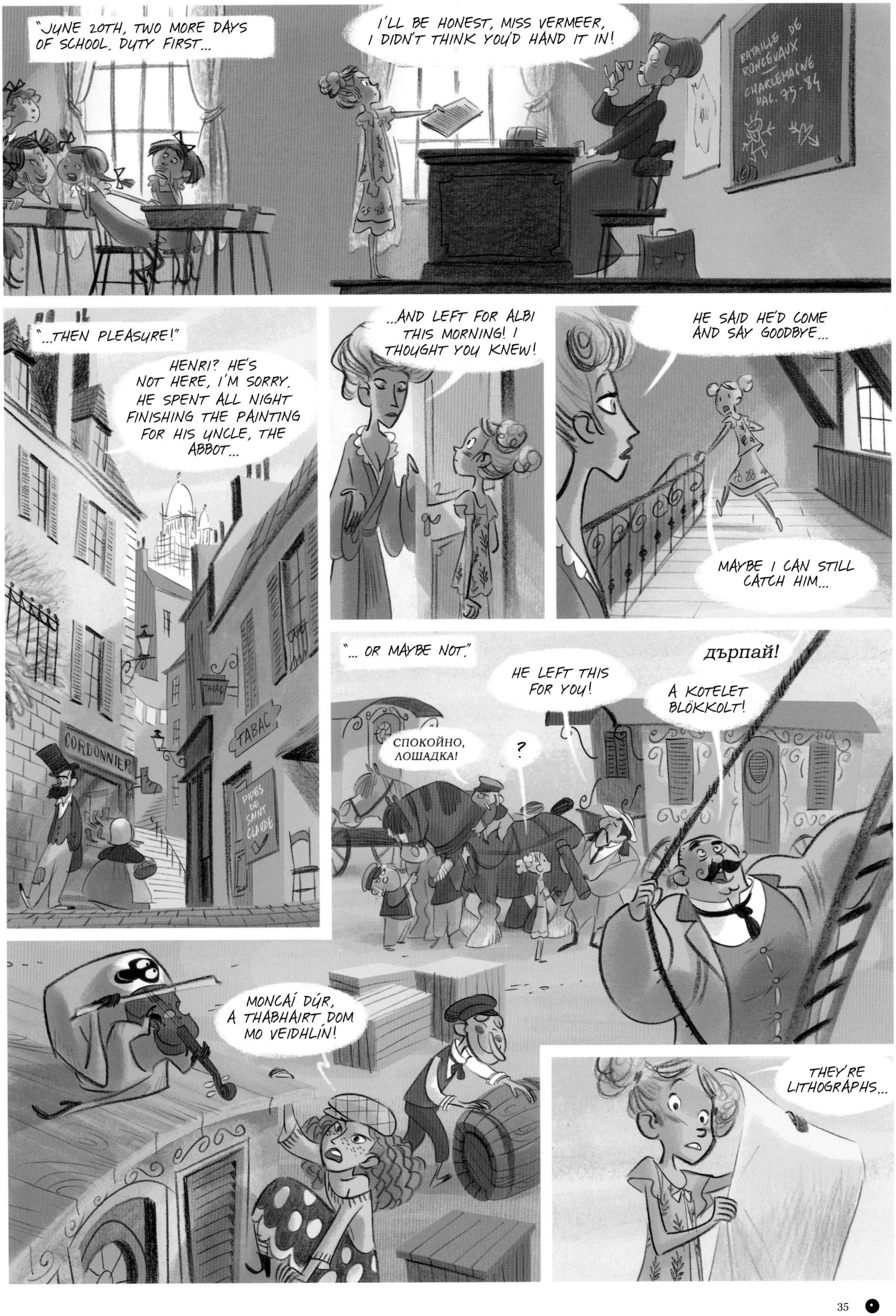
"JUNE 20TH, TWO MORE DAYS OF SCHOOL. DUTY FIRST...
I'LL BE HONEST, MISS VERMEER, I DIDN'T THINK YOU'D HAND IT IN!
BATAILLE DE RONCEVAUX CHARLEMAGNE PAG. 75-84
"...THEN PLEASURE!"
HENRI? HE'S NOT HERE, I'M SORRY. HE SPENT ALL NIGHT FINISHING THE PAINTING FOR HIS UNCLE, THE ABBOT...
...AND LEFT FOR ALBI THIS MORNING! I THOUGHT YOU KNEW!
HE SAID HE'D COME AND SAY GOODBYE...
MAYBE I CAN STILL CATCH HIM...
CORDONNIER
TABAC
PIPES DE SAINT CLAUDE
"... OR MAYBE NOT."
дърпай!
HE LEFT THIS FOR YOU!
A KOTELET BLÖKKOLT!
СПОКОЙНО, ЛОШАДКА!
?
MONCAÍ DÚR, A THABHAIRT DOM MO VEIDHLÍN!
THEY'RE LITHOGRAPHS...

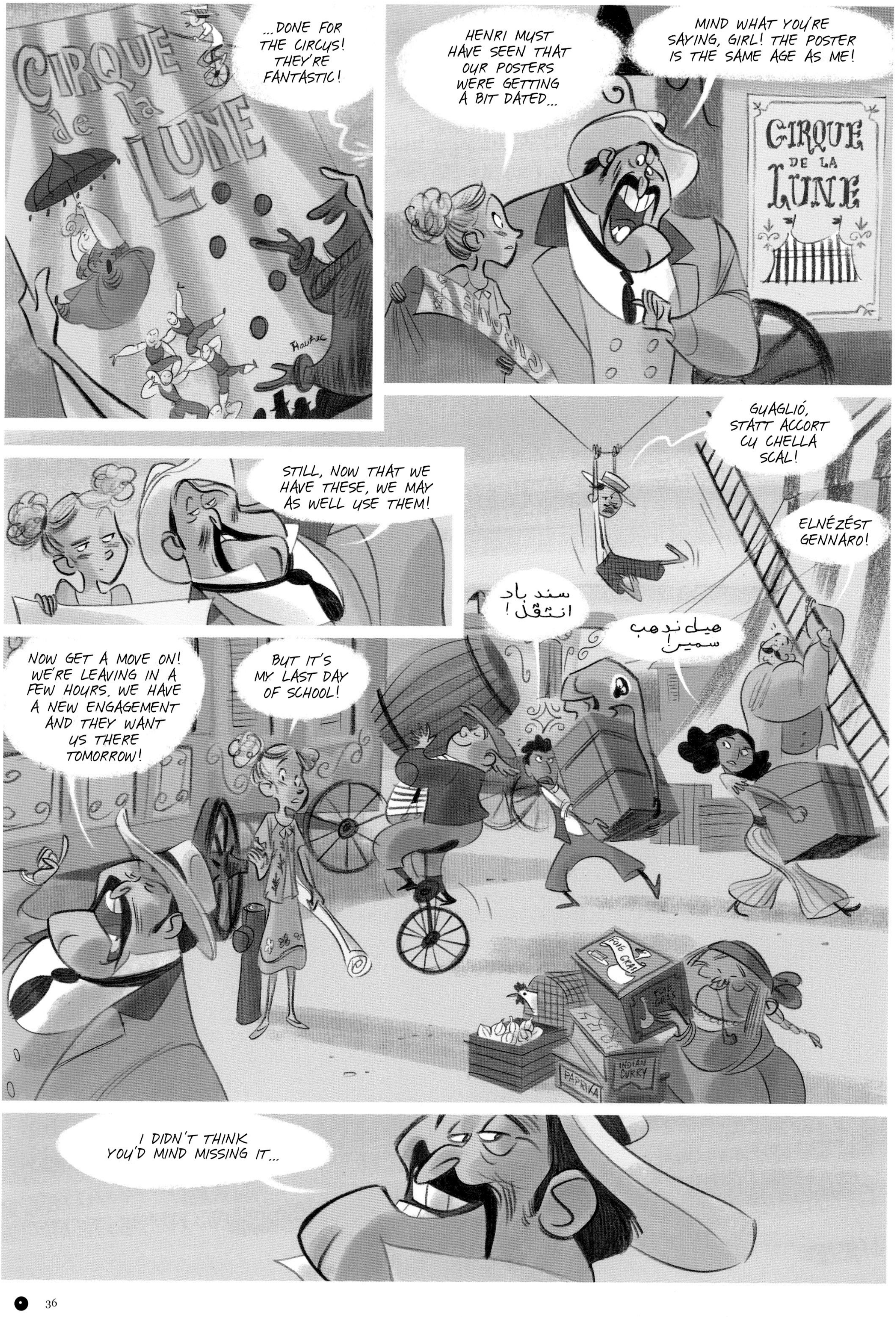
CIRQUE de la LUNE
...DONE FOR THE CIRCUS! THEY'RE FANTASTIC!
HENRI MUST HAVE SEEN THAT OUR POSTERS WERE GETTING A BIT DATED...
MIND WHAT YOU'RE SAYING, GIRL! THE POSTER IS THE SAME AGE AS ME!
CIRQUE DE LA LUNE
STILL, NOW THAT WE HAVE THESE, WE MAY AS WELL USE THEM!
GUAGLIÓ, STATT ACCORT CU CHELLA SCAL!
ELNÉZÉST GENNARO!
سند باد انتقل!
هيك ندهب سمير!
NOW GET A MOVE ON! WE'RE LEAVING IN A FEW HOURS. WE HAVE A NEW ENGAGEMENT AND THEY WANT US THERE TOMORROW!
BUT IT'S MY LAST DAY OF SCHOOL!
FOIE GRAS
FOIE GRAS
INDIAN CURRY
PAPRIKA
I DIDN'T THINK YOU'D MIND MISSING IT...

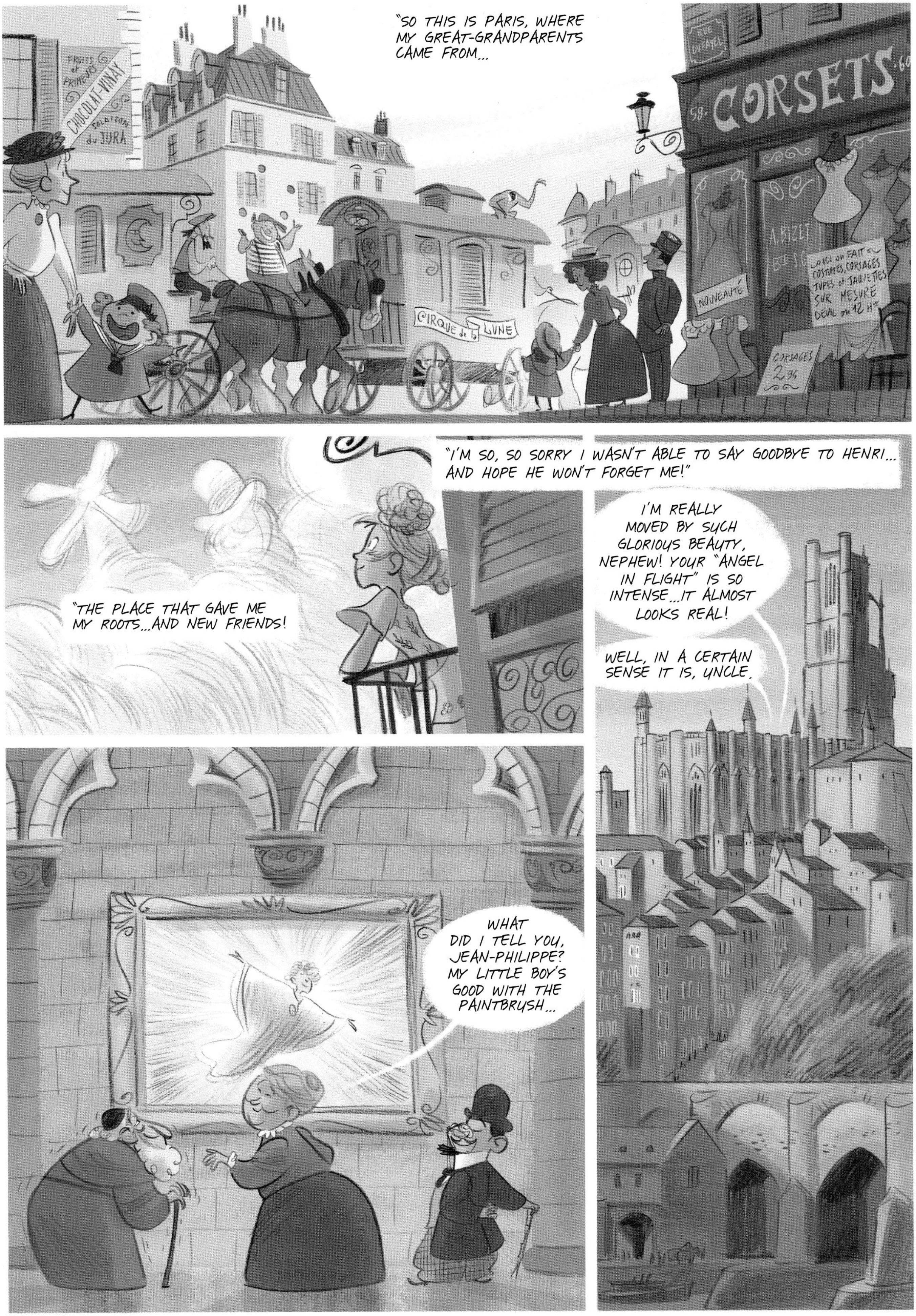
"SO THIS IS PARIS, WHERE MY GREAT-GRANDPARENTS CAME FROM...
FRUITS et PRIMEURS
CHOCOLAT-VINAY
SALAISON du JURA
RUE DUFAYEL
58. CORSETS
A. BIZET
NOUVEAUTÉ
CIRQUE de la LUNE
CORSAGES
"I'M SO, SO SORRY I WASN'T ABLE TO SAY GOODBYE TO HENRI... AND HOPE HE WON'T FORGET ME!"
"THE PLACE THAT GAVE ME MY ROOTS... AND NEW FRIENDS!
I'M REALLY MOVED BY SUCH GLORIOUS BEAUTY, NEPHEW! YOUR "ANGEL IN FLIGHT" IS SO INTENSE... IT ALMOST LOOKS REAL!
WELL, IN A CERTAIN SENSE IT IS, UNCLE.
WHAT DID I TELL YOU, JEAN-PHILIPPE? MY LITTLE BOY'S GOOD WITH THE PAINTBRUSH...

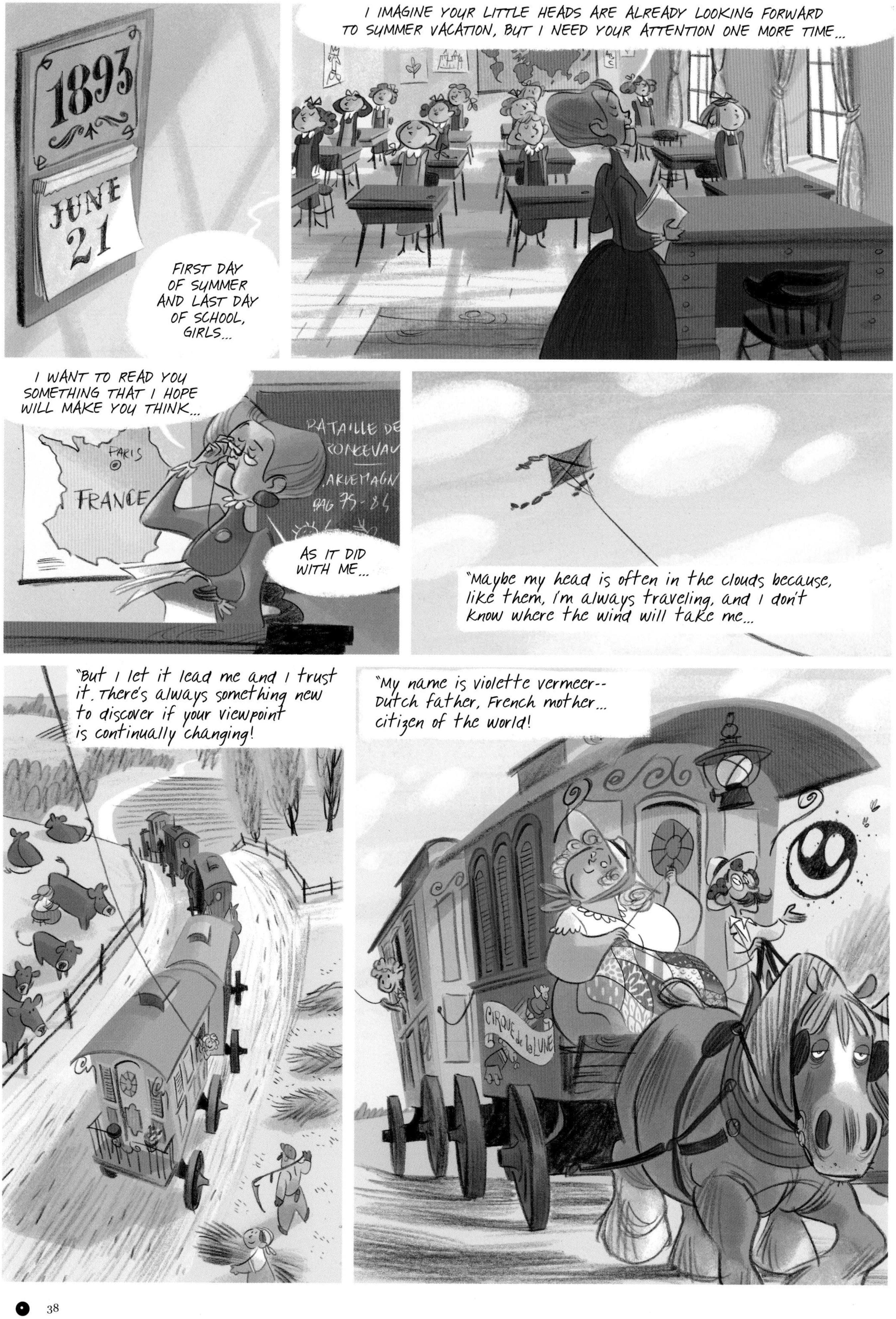
1893
JUNE 21
I IMAGINE YOUR LITTLE HEADS ARE ALREADY LOOKING FORWARD TO SUMMER VACATION, BUT I NEED YOUR ATTENTION ONE MORE TIME...
FIRST DAY OF SUMMER AND LAST DAY OF SCHOOL, GIRLS...
I WANT TO READ YOU SOMETHING THAT I HOPE WILL MAKE YOU THINK...
PARIS
FRANCE
AS IT DID WITH ME...
"Maybe my head is often in the clouds because, like them, I'm always traveling, and I don't know where the wind will take me...
"But I let it lead me and I trust it. There's always something new to discover if your viewpoint is continually changing!
"My name is Violette Vermeer-- Dutch father, French mother... citizen of the world!
CIRQUE de la LUNE

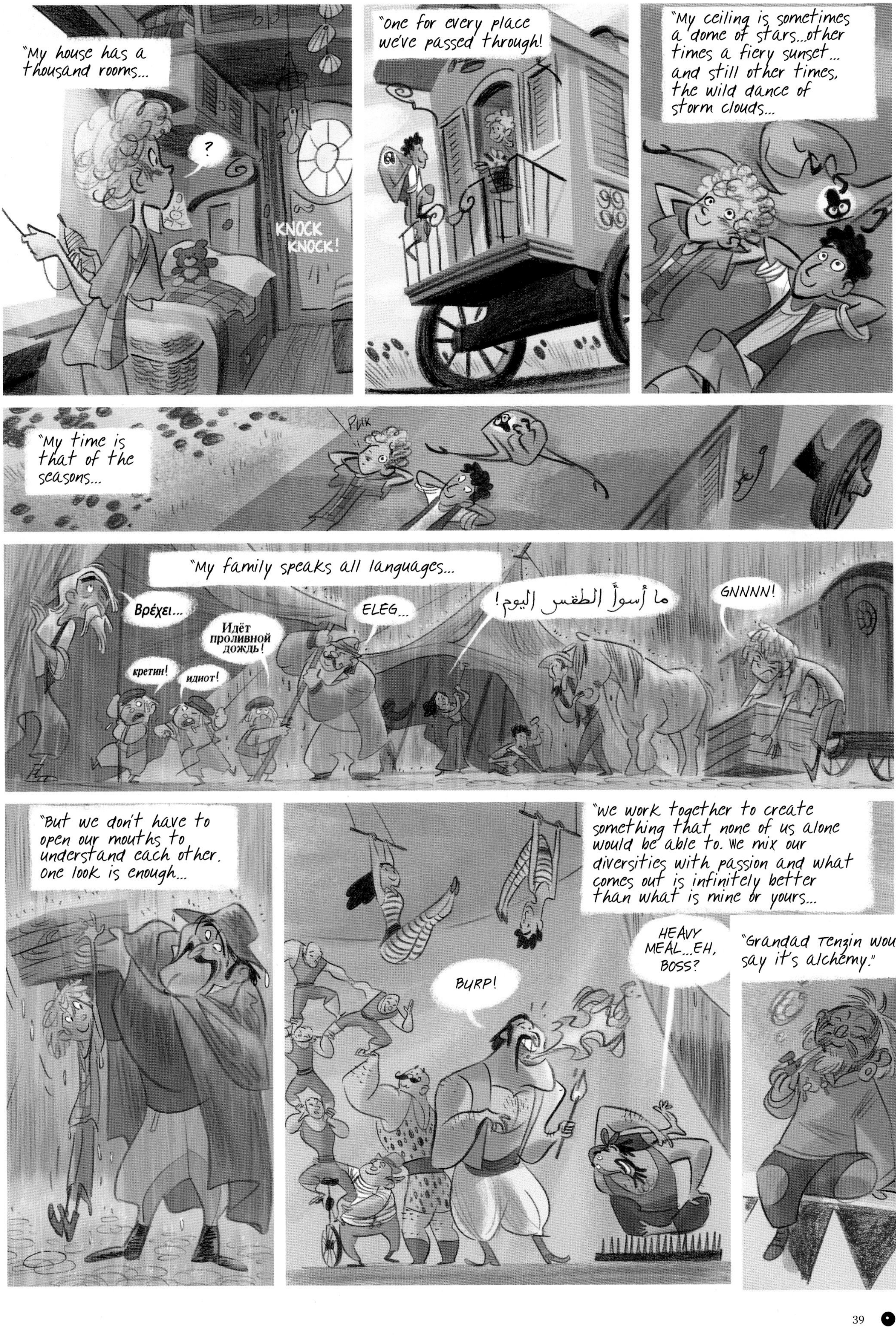

"My house has a thousand rooms...
?
KNOCK KNOCK!
"one for every place we've passed through!
"My ceiling is sometimes a dome of stars...other times a fiery sunset... and still other times, the wild dance of storm clouds...
"My time is that of the seasons...
PLIK
"My family speaks all languages...
Βρέχει...
кретин!
идиот!
Идёт проливной дождь!
ELEG...
ما أسوأ الطقس اليوم!
GNNNN!
"But we don't have to open our mouths to understand each other. One look is enough...
"we work together to create something that none of us alone would be able to. We mix our diversities with passion and what comes out is infinitely better than what is mine or yours...
BURP!
HEAVY MEAL...EH, BOSS?
"Grandad Tenzin would say it's alchemy."

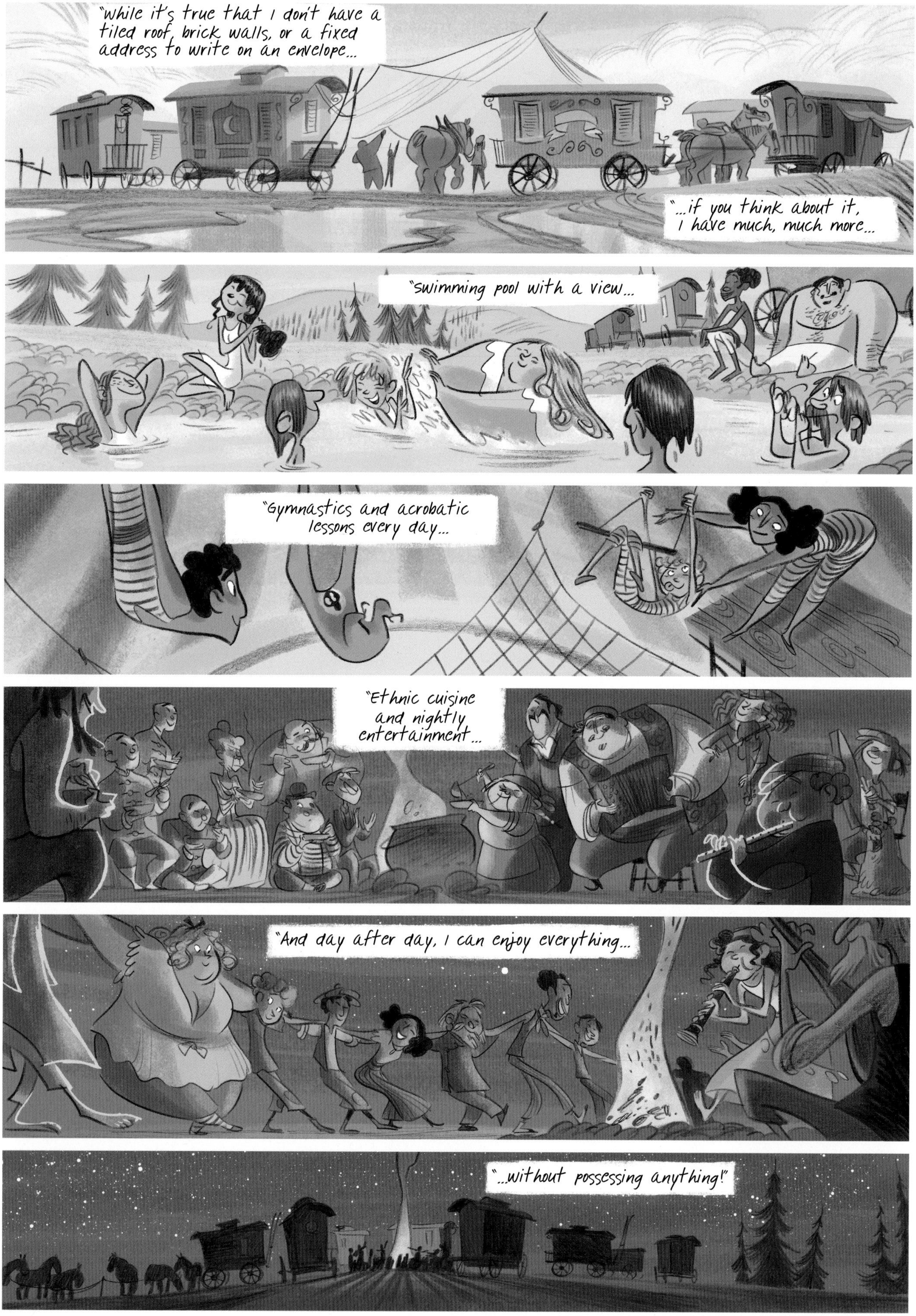
"While it's true that I don't have a tiled roof, brick walls, or a fixed address to write on an envelope...
"...if you think about it, I have much, much more...
"Swimming pool with a view...
"Gymnastics and acrobatic lessons every day...
"Ethnic cuisine and nightly entertainment...
"And day after day, I can enjoy everything...
"...without possessing anything!"

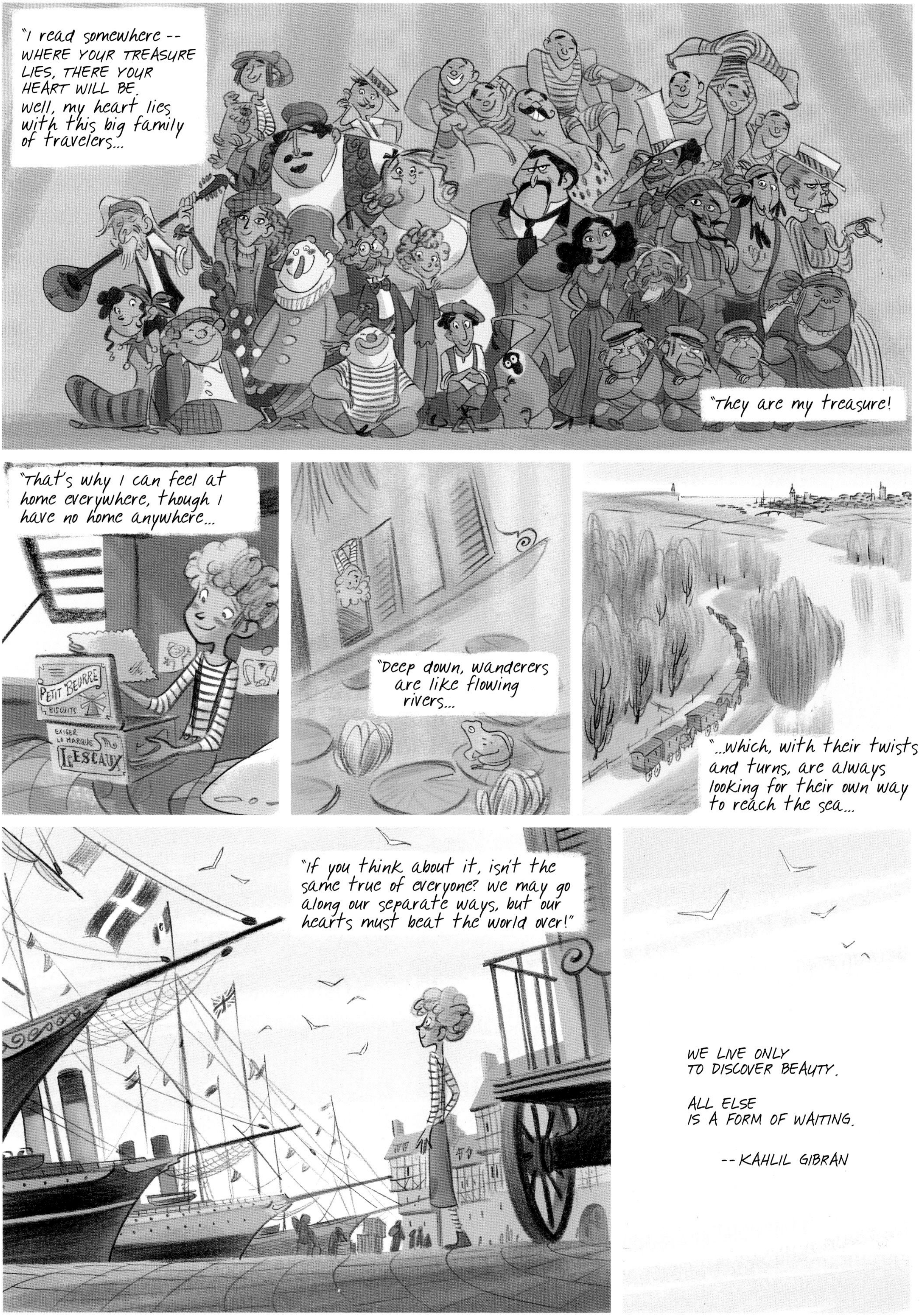
"I read somewhere -- WHERE YOUR TREASURE LIES, THERE YOUR HEART WILL BE. Well, my heart lies with this big family of travelers...
"They are my treasure!
"That's why I can feel at home everywhere, though I have no home anywhere...
PETIT BEURRE
BISCUITS
EXIGER LA MARQUE
LESCAUX
"Deep down, wanderers are like flowing rivers...
"...which, with their twists and turns, are always looking for their own way to reach the sea...
"If you think about it, isn't the same true of everyone? We may go along our separate ways, but our hearts must beat the world over!"
WE LIVE ONLY TO DISCOVER BEAUTY.
ALL ELSE IS A FORM OF WAITING.
-- KAHLIL GIBRAN

Henri de Toulouse-Lautrec (1864-1901) really existed! He is one of the great French painters of the late Nineteenth Century— during what's called the post-Impressionist period. His most famous paintings are those where he sketched the essence of the Montmartre section in Paris—the cabaret life of the Moulin Rouge and its famous dancers.

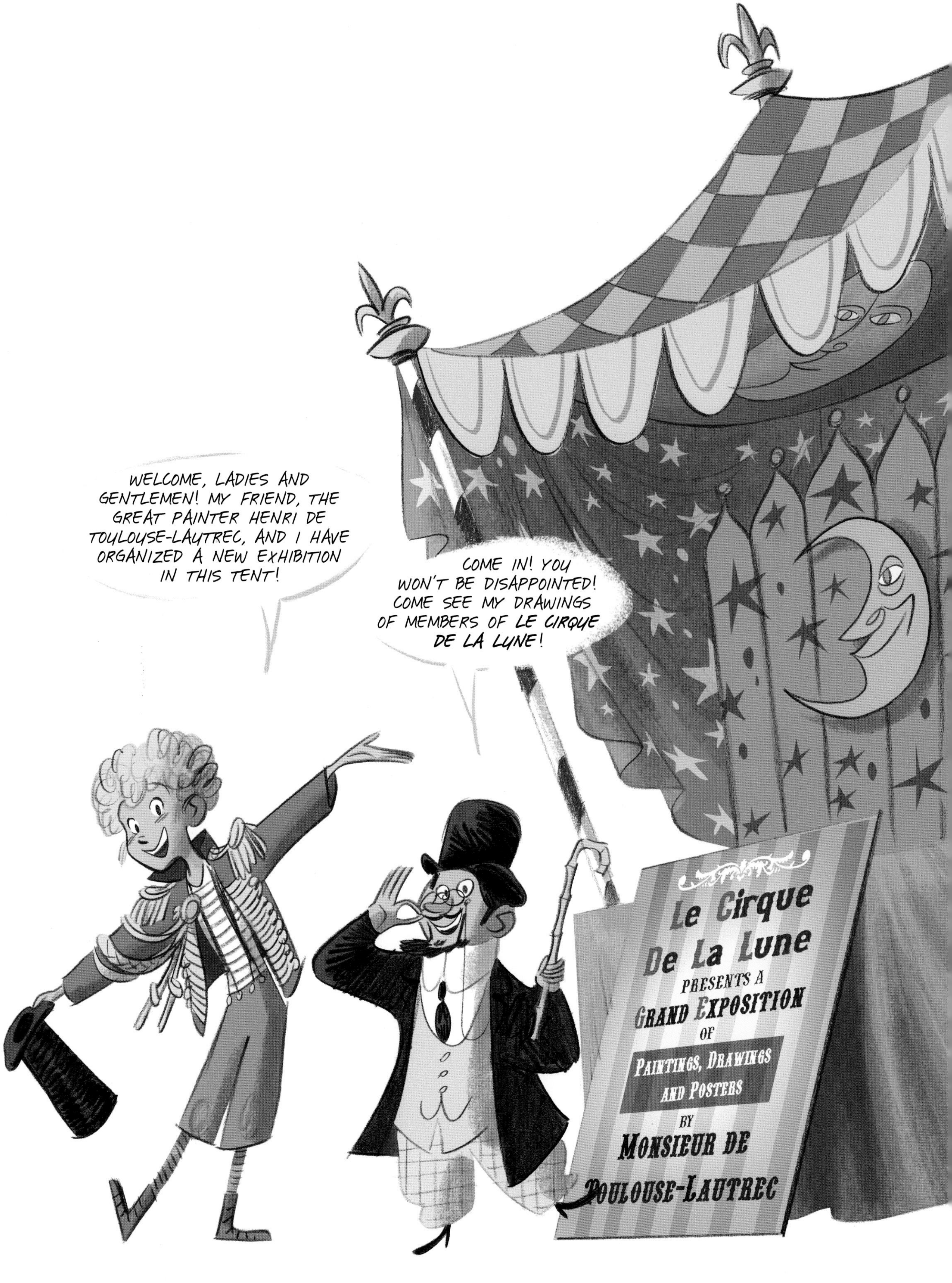
WELCOME, LADIES AND GENTLEMEN! MY FRIEND, THE GREAT PAINTER HENRI DE TOULOUSE-LAUTREC, AND I HAVE ORGANIZED A NEW EXHIBITION IN THIS TENT!
COME IN! YOU WON'T BE DISAPPOINTED! COME SEE MY DRAWINGS OF MEMBERS OF LE CIRQUE DE LA LUNE!
Le Cirque De La Lune PRESENTS A GRAND EXPOSITION OF PAINTINGS, DRAWINGS AND POSTERS BY MONSIEUR DE TOULOUSE-LAUTREC

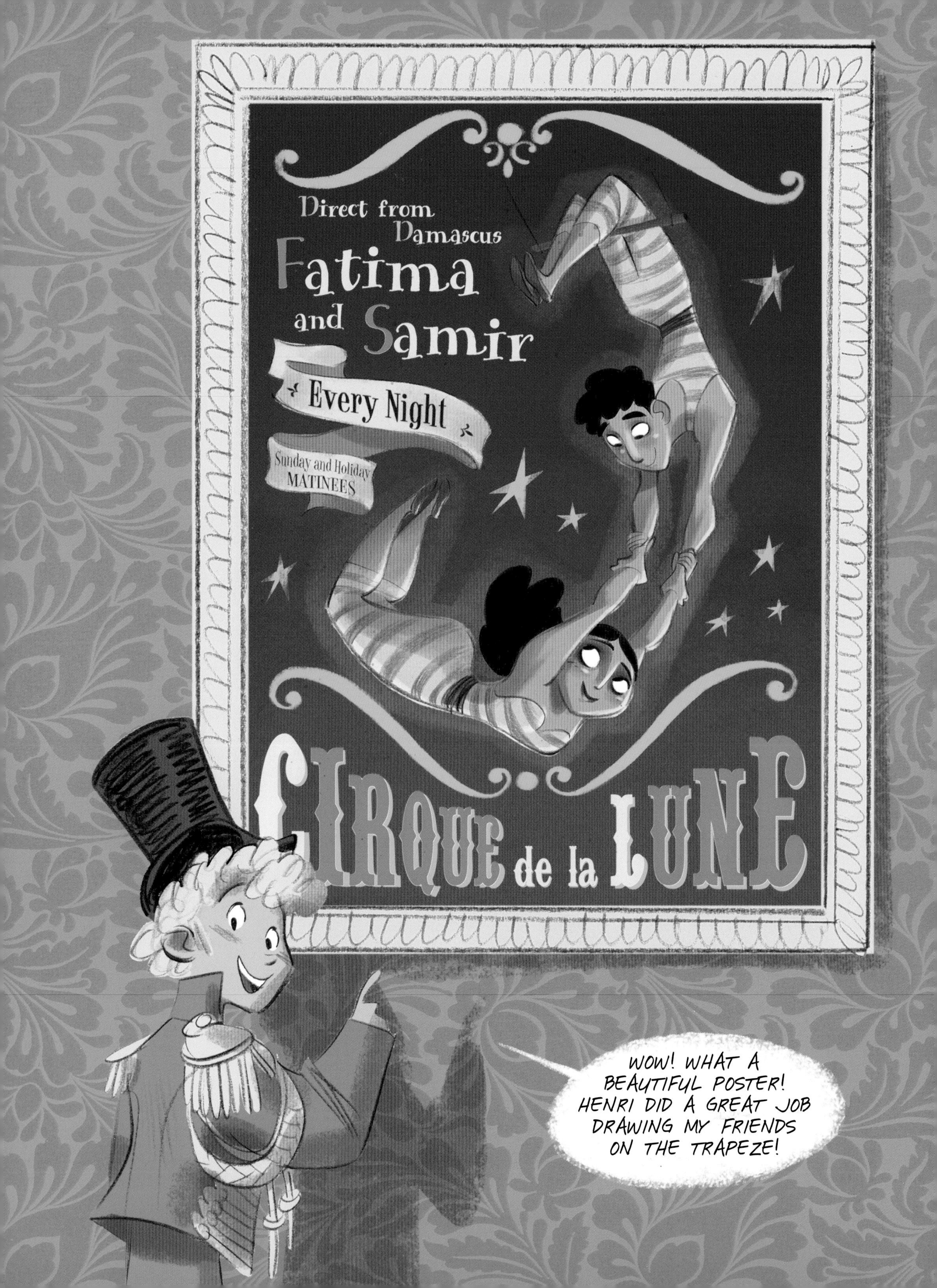
Direct from Damascus
Fatima and Samir
Every Night
Sunday and Holiday MATINEES
CIRQUE de la LUNE
WOW! WHAT A BEAUTIFUL POSTER! HENRI DID A GREAT JOB DRAWING MY FRIENDS ON THE TRAPEZE!

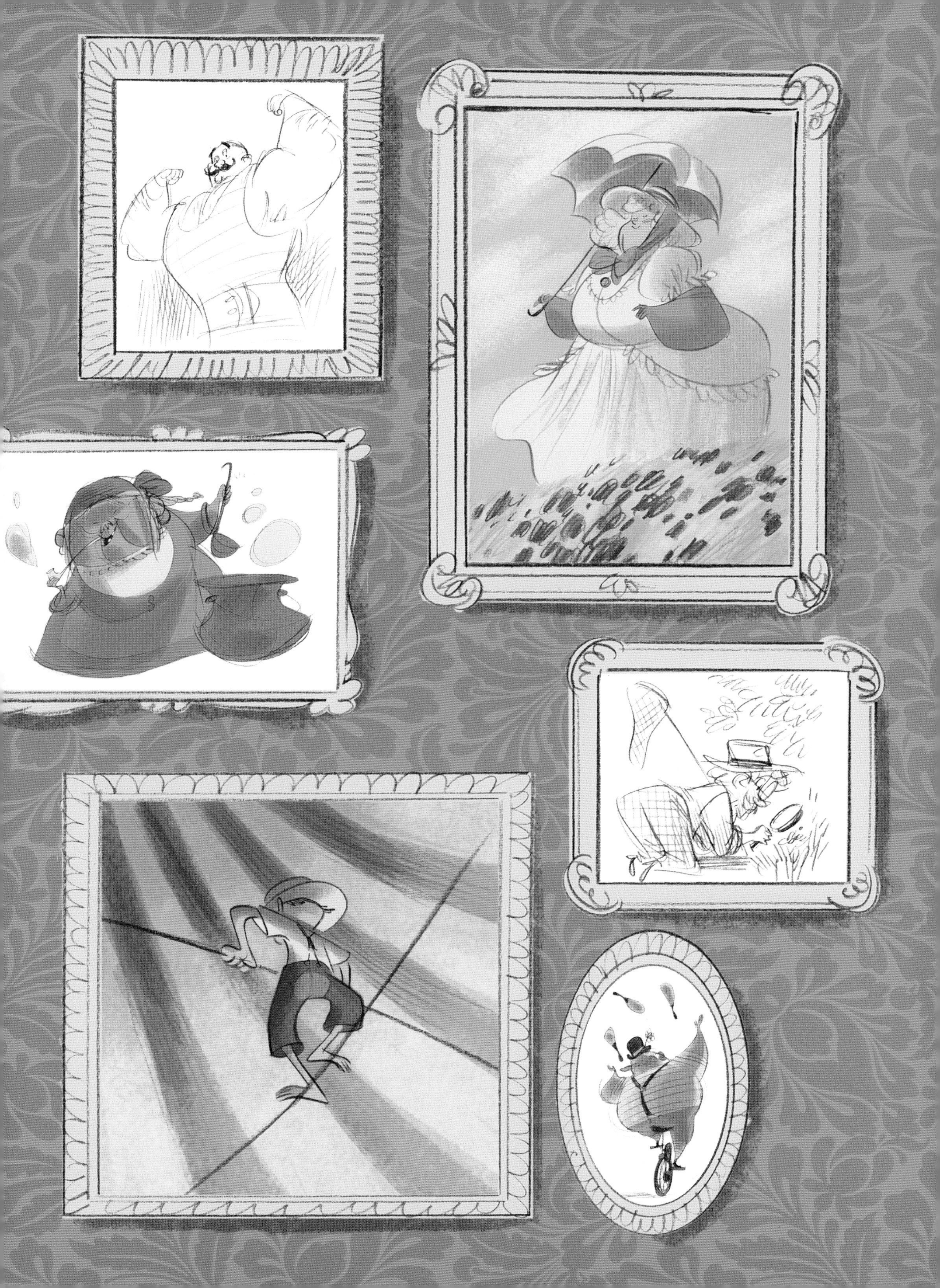

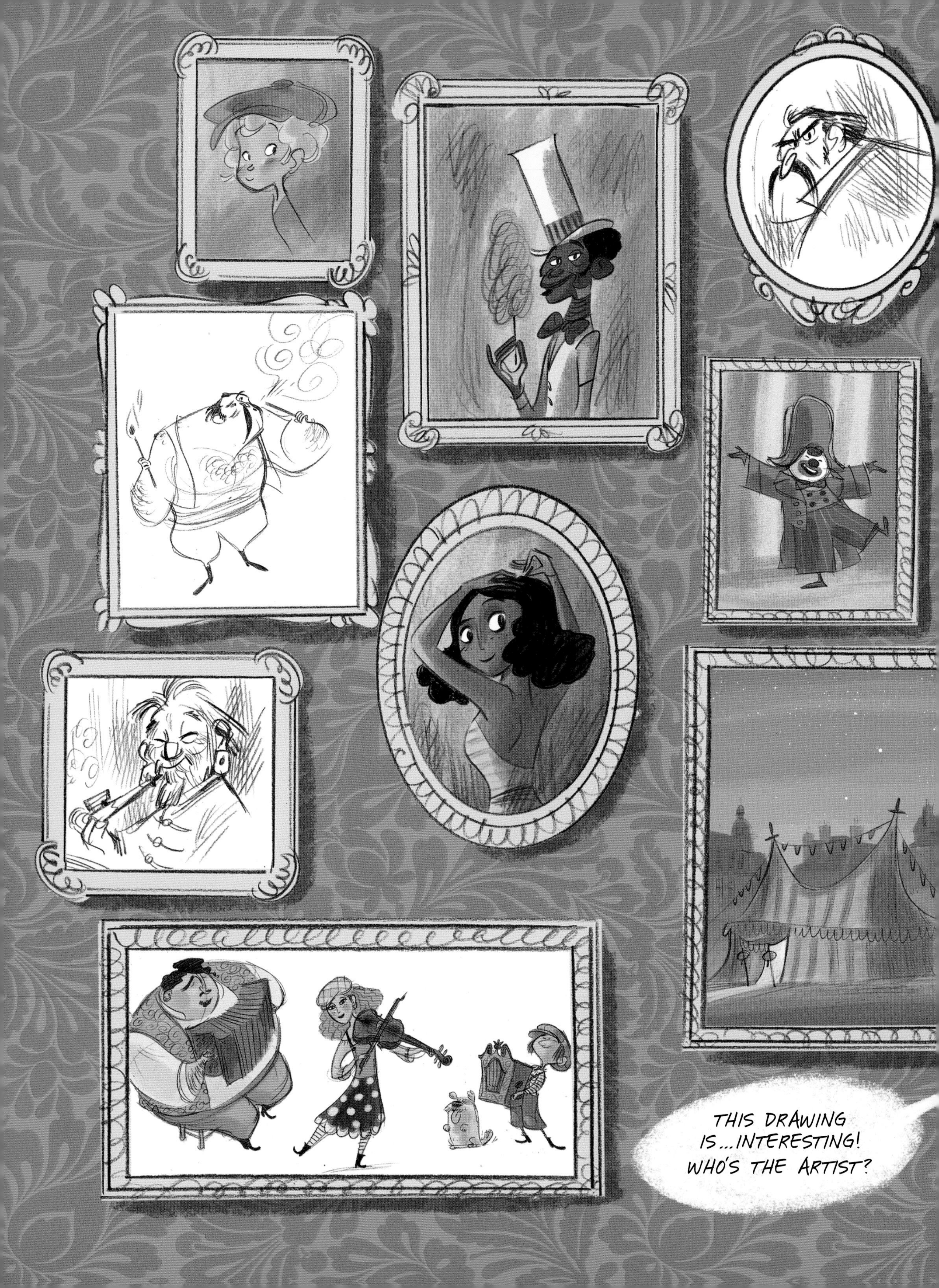
THIS DRAWING IS...INTERESTING! WHO'S THE ARTIST?

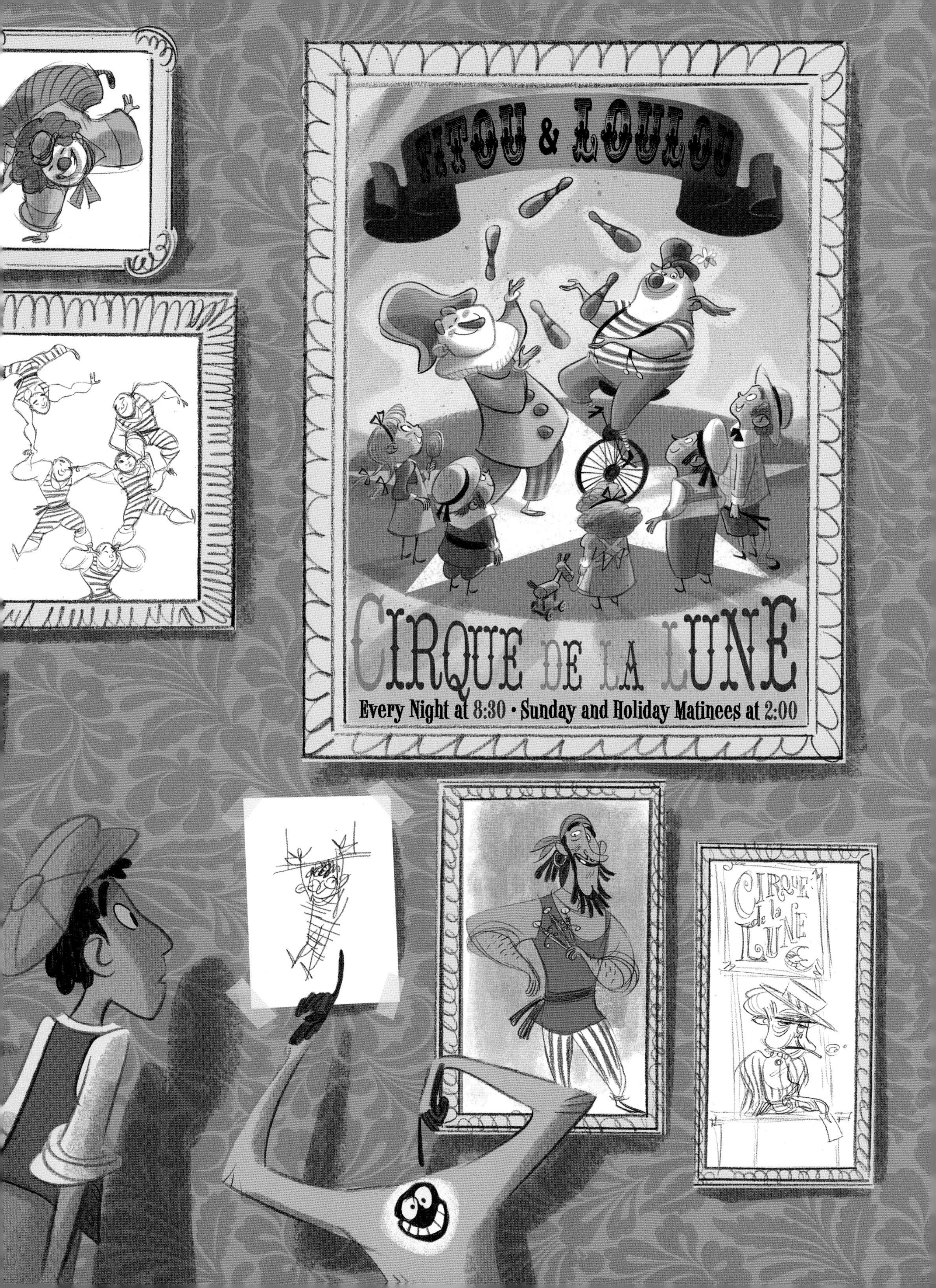
TITOU & LOULOU
CIRQUE DE LA LUNE
Every Night at 8:30 • Sunday and Holiday Matinees at 2:00
CIRQUE de la LUNE

Script:
Teresa Radice

Illustrations and Colors:
Stefano Turconi

Translation by Terrence Chamberlain   Edited by Dean Mullaney

TO TATINA,
NAMED AFTER A FLOWER, A COLOR, AND AN INSTRUMENT--
LOOK ONLY FOR BEAUTY, LOVE LIFE AND OTHERS, and NEVER
STOP BEING AMAZED AT NATURE, ART, MUSIC...MANKIND.

AND TO ELA,
YOU ALWAYS LOVED EVERY ONE OF OUR STORIES...
AND YOU WERE WAITING FOR THIS ONE. NOW YOU'RE
BACK HOME, WE'RE SENDING IT WITH ALL OUR LOVE.

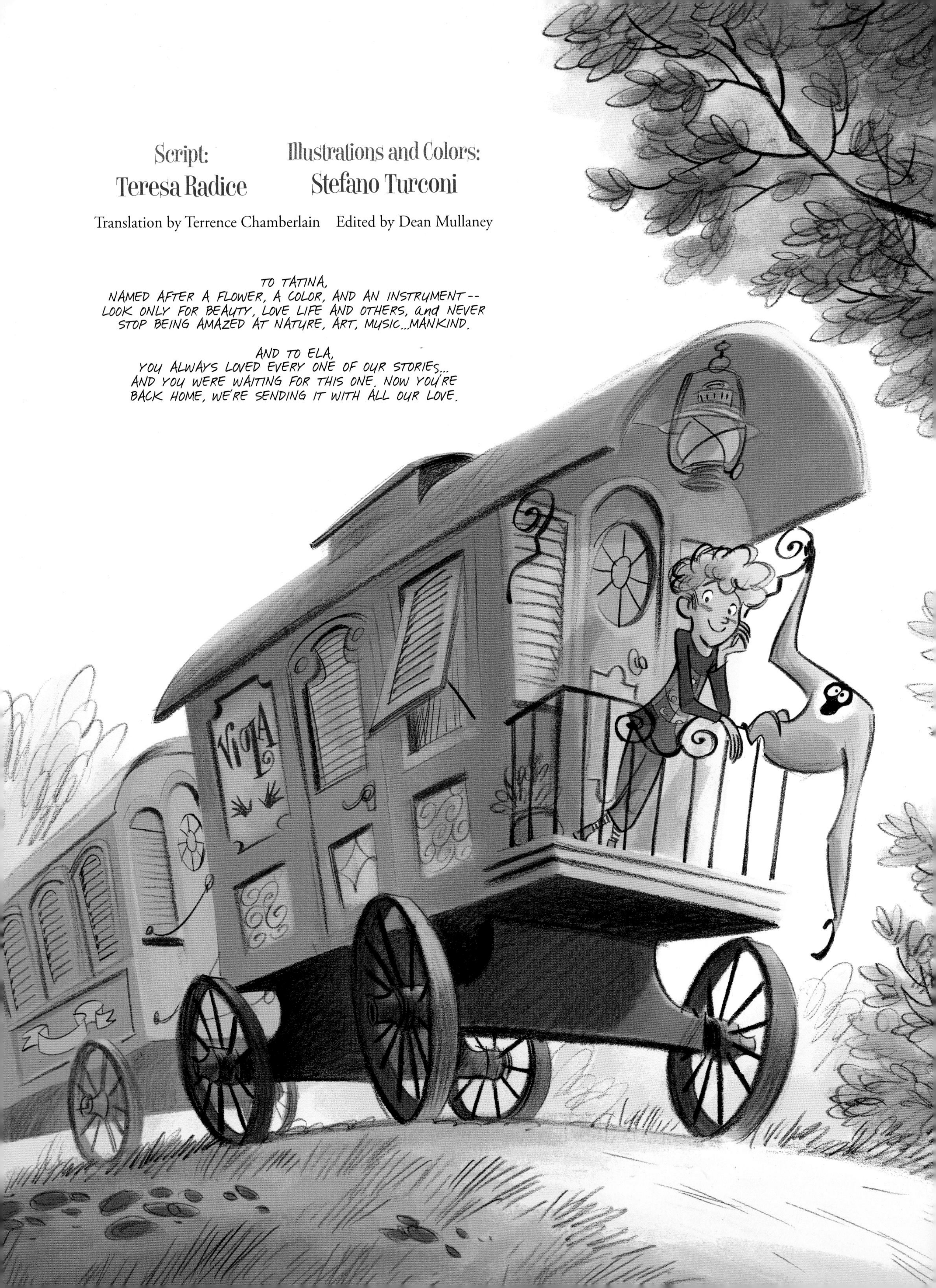
VIOLA

Text and illustrations © 2013 Teresa Radice - Stefano Turconi - Tunué.
Originally published in Italy as *Viola giramondo* by Tunué. All rights reserved.
Published by arrangement with Mediatoon Licensing/Tunué.
Cover design from the French edition, published by Dargaud.

EuroComics.us

Dean Mullaney, CREATIVE DIRECTOR • Lorraine Turner, ART DIRECTOR

EuroComics is an imprint of IDW Publishing,
a Division of Idea and Design Works, LLC
2765 Truxtun Road, San Diego, CA 92106 • www.idwpublishing.com

Distributed to the book trade by Penguin Random House
Distributed to the comic book trade by Diamond Book Distributors

ISBN: 978-1-68405-188-5 • First Printing, March 2018

IDW Publishing
Greg Goldstein, President & Publisher
Robbie Robbins, EVP & Sr. Art Director
Chris Ryall, Chief Creative Officer & Editor-in-Chief
Matthew Ruzicka, CPA, Chief Financial Officer
David Hedgecock, Associate Publisher
Laurie Windrow, Senior Vice President of Sales & Marketing
Lorelei Bunjes, VP of Digital Services
Eric Moss, Sr. Director, Licensing & Business Development

Ted Adams, Founder & CEO of IDW Media Holdings

Special thanks to Sophie Castille and Émilie Védis at Mediatoons, Cecilia Raneri at Tunué,
Justin Eisinger, Alonzo Simon, and Edward Gauvin.

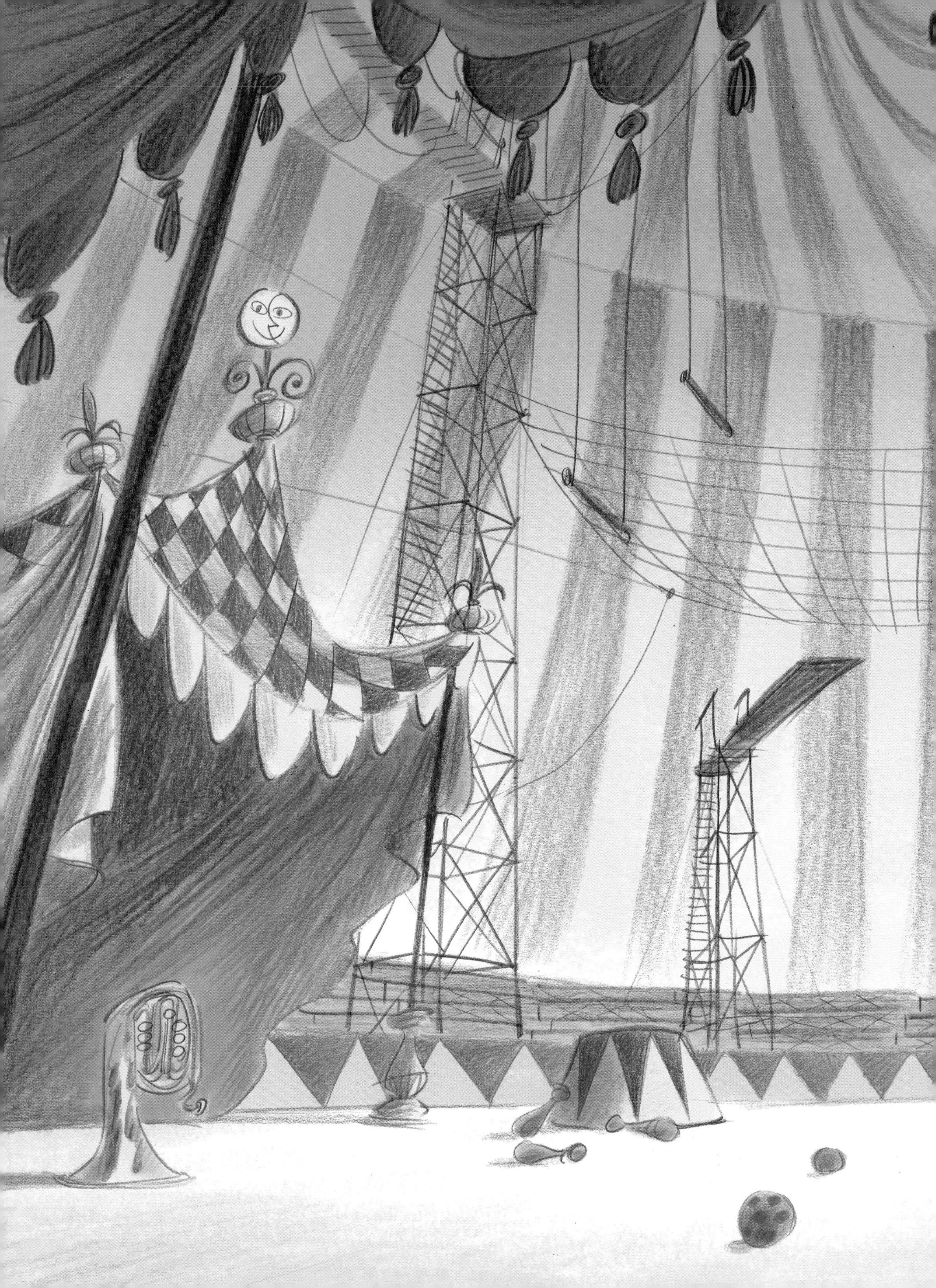